I0774613

H7N9

Escape

The H7N9 Chronicles Book 2

Mark Campbell

This is a work of fiction.

Names, characters, businesses, places, events, locales, and incidents are the products of the author's imagination or used fictitiously. Any resemblance to actual persons, living or dead, or actual events is purely coincidental.

Copyright © 2024 Mark Campbell

Cover design by Adam Hay Studio, UK
Author: Mark Campbell
Edited by: Katelynn W.
Published by: Darkest Hour, Houston, TX

ISBN: 979-8-9910532-3-5

PROLOGUE

NOVEMBER 4th

Los Angeles was burning.

Flames crept over the Hollywood Hills, leaving smoldering mansions and charred remnants of palms, cypress, and jacaranda trees. The fire spread to the sprawling city, its orange glow reflecting off skyscrapers through the murky haze. Thick black smoke obscured the sun, and gray ash fluttered from the sky like snow. Embers carried by the breeze threatened to ignite smaller fires deeper in the city.

Miles away, safe at an estate high in the Santa Monica Mountains, Senator Mark Hammond sipped cognac and watched the fire from his study window. The stale odor of cigar smoke clung to his tuxedo.

As he watched, he speculated on what could have ignited the blaze. Nights were cooling, and electricity was unreliable. Had someone left an appliance running before the flu worsened? Had a campfire gotten out of control? Or was it a simple cigarette butt tossed out a car window?

Regardless, he knew it would spread. Storms had been absent as of late, and that summer had been especially dry. Hammond took another sip. The fire would soon reach Beverly Hills, climb the mountainside, and devour the remaining estates there. It was only a matter of time. Soon, he and the others would have to venture into the unknown.

The study was one of the home's more ostentatiously decorated rooms. Mahogany bookcases towered over Persian rugs. Seventeenth-century oil paintings surrounded the handmade desk. A crystal chandelier bathed the room in soft, white light. He didn't care for the ornate décor, but he valued the literature he'd amassed—thousands of books filled his shelves. Hammond felt sorrow for the books that would soon turn into ash. He had never read many of the books in his collection, using them solely for decoration.

He sighed, swirled the cognac remaining in the snifter, and continued studying the burning city through the picture window.

There was an urgent knock at the study door; Hammond invited the visitor in without turning around.

The door opened, letting in laughter and classical music. A young man in a black suit with a clear, coiled earpiece in one ear peered at Hammond from the doorway.

"Sir, we've been given orders to leave."

"I figured as much," the senator replied before he took another sip. "When will our transport be here?"

"Ten minutes, give or take. We have to go by ground because of the smoke, but the freeway is clear. They bulldozed a path through the abandoned cars there this morning."

"Go by ground?" the senator asked, frowning. "During a wildfire?"

"Yes, sir. The fire hasn't crossed the freeway to the convention center. The wind is picking up, though."

"Fine," the senator grumbled. "Let me finish my drink. I'll be out momentarily."

"Yes, sir." The agent stepped back outside and closed the door.

"What a mess," Hammond said to himself. Just as he raised his glass to finish the cognac, another knock interrupted him. He scowled and lowered the glass. "I said to give me a moment!"

Heedless of his words, the door opened to reveal a short, husky man in an ill-fitting suit and a top hat. His cheeks flushed from too much wine, and he laughed boisterously at the sight that greeted him.

"Someone is in a rather sour mood!" he declared.

Startled, Hammond turned to face the newcomer, who just so happened to be the head of one of the nation's largest banking firms. He had lined the senator's pockets significantly during the last, and possibly final, election.

"Mr. Weinberg, I apologize. I thought you were with my security detail."

"I suppose you heard the news, then." Weinberg waddled to the desk and plopped down with a heavy sigh.

"Unfortunately, yes." The senator turned away from the window, placed his glass on the desk, and took a seat opposite Weinberg. "How are the others taking it?"

"Most are too liquored up to care. The rest think we'll be whisked away to another deserted mansion." Weinberg grinned and waved his hand dismissively. "The band hasn't even stopped playing!"

"I don't think we'll be heading somewhere fancy this time." Hammond glanced out the window, then frowned at a letter on his desk. "I think we're finally headed to the promised land."

While waiting out the pandemic in San Francisco, an army officer delivered the letter to Hammond before they shuttled him off with other wealthy politicians and people of influence.

Weinberg drummed his fingers against his chin. "Do you think the facilities are ready?"

"Doubtful." Hammond closed his eyes, folded his hands over his chest, and leaned back in his chair. "If they could, they'd stash us somewhere else and buy more time. Something tells me they're desperate."

Weinberg grabbed the letter. "Is this the invitation?"

"I wouldn't call it an invitation, but yes, that's what they gave me before they grabbed me."

Weinberg narrowed his eyes and scanned the letter. "Department of Homeland Security: mandatory civilian conscription notice. Under Article I, Section 8 of the United States Constitution, 10 US Code Section 246, and under the full scope and authority of the US Presidential Policy Directive 40 Continuity of Operations Protocol, you have been selected to serve as the director of operations at one of our facilities for a period yet to be determined based on the needs of whichever region you will be assigned. As a token of appreciation for your service, we will offer you one of the many vacant Cabinet positions within the new government once the recovery period concludes. Monetary compensation will be discussed once the economy has been reestablished. You and your family are required to surrender immediately to custody for medical screening, and—" Weinberg stopped reading and crumpled the letter before tossing it over his shoulder with a snort. "It's the same canned garbage they sent me. When they delivered it, they led me away like I was some sort of criminal! Do you think they'll even keep their promises?"

"I think so," Hammond said with a shrug. "If they were going to bamboozle us, they wouldn't have shuffled us around like this and given us such extensive security. They would've stuck us in one of those awful quarantine centers with everyone else."

"I guess you're right. I never took you as an optimist."

"On the contrary," Hammond said, "I believe all of this is going to end badly. I don't think they'll be able to rebuild Babylon."

"Then why go along with it at all?" Weinberg asked.

Hammond mulled over the question for a moment, his gaze focused on his glass before moving to the shiny, gold wedding band on his finger. "I guess I'm in it for the drinks." He gulped down the last swig of cognac and slammed the empty glass on the desk. "If they send us to another castle in the hills, I hope the owner has some cognac stashed away."

Weinberg chuckled, his hands resting on his oversized belly. Hammond stared down at his wedding band again and started rolling it around on his finger. Weinberg's smile faded as his eyes trailed down to where Hammond fiddled with the ring.

"Say, you never told me—and I feel like a heel for not asking—what happened to Laura? Was she—?"

A tremor shook the house. In the other room, the band finally stopped playing. There was a collective gasp from the guests as the estate went dark. Hammond glanced up at the chandelier. A few seconds later, the generators turned on again, and the lights came back to life.

"We should start heading out," Hammond announced, then stood and dusted bits of fallen plaster off his shoulders. "It sounds like the party is over."

"Right," Weinberg said before clearing his throat. He forced himself out of the chair, hiked up his pants, and adjusted his top hat. "I'll meet you downstairs with the others."

"See you shortly," Hammond said.

Weinberg nodded and waddled out of the room. Two agents carrying submachine guns appeared in the doorway as soon as he was gone.

"Sir, we need to leave right now," one of them said. "The fire is compromising the southern support pillars and spreading to the generator room. Join the others outside at the transport."

"I'm coming." With his back turned to the agents, Hammond reached up and wiped away the tears that Laura's memory brought to his eyes.

The two men disappeared down the hallway. Not thirty seconds later, another tremor shook the house, and the lights went out again.

Hammond turned to leave, but then paused and gazed at his wedding band again in the gloom. With a trembling hand, he slid it off his finger and dropped it into the empty glass.

1

NOVEMBER 23rd

The overhead lights flickered, and the luggage bins rattled as Amtrak's California Zephyr sped westward. Cold air blasted through the vents, keeping the carriage uncomfortably chilly. Passengers drifted in and out of sleep, their heads knocking from side to side with each turn. Those fortunate enough to have a companion huddled together for warmth and comfort. Most, however, were alone as they faced an unknown destination.

The tight-lipped officials had offered no new information since the train pulled out of Tucson hours earlier. Teddy Sanders slouched in his seat with his arms crossed. His back ached, and his legs were numb. The stench of unwashed bodies—including his own—filled the carriage. He thought his nose would grow accustomed to the smell, but maybe that was just wishful thinking.

Early morning sunlight poured through the windows, casting an orange haze through the dusty air. Teddy's window shutter was pulled down, so he did not know what the view was like or where the train was headed. Wherever it was, he doubted it would be good.

On the seat next to him, Ein, his chin resting on his chest, snored. His messy, purple hair hung around his face, a string of drool clinging to his lip. His clothes were in no better shape than Teddy's; white spots covered his black T-shirt, and his faded black jeans were ripped at the knees.

The door at the front of the carriage slid open, and a FEMA officer entered. He carried an assault rifle and wore a ballistic helmet; the word

POLICE was emblazoned on his vest. As he walked down the aisle, checking passengers, a garbled voice came over his Motorola radio.

"—is critical and already low on supplies."

The officer lowered the radio's volume and disappeared through the door to the next carriage.

The carriage jerked, jolting everyone inside. Ein's head lolled to the side and rested on Teddy's shoulder until Teddy pushed him away.

Ein woke with a start. "What happened?"

"You were doing it again."

"Sorry." Ein yawned, rubbing his neck. "It's hard to get comfortable in seats that don't recline."

"I'd rather you sleep than do that nervous fidgeting thing you did for the first four hours."

"Can you blame me for being nervous?" Ein's gaze darted between the carriage doors.

"You're going to have to hold it together," Teddy replied. "If the others smell fear or sense weakness, you might as well have a target on your back."

"Is that some more helpful advice from your previous life?"

Teddy glared at his traveling companion, regretting having divulged so much to someone he hardly knew. It was a mistake he normally didn't make.

"Keep that to yourself," he whispered. "If the wrong person hears your smart-ass comments, I'll be the one in trouble."

Ein looked down, squirming in his seat. "You're right. I'm sorry."

"And stop apologizing so much!" Teddy turned to the darkened screen mounted on the headrest in front of him. "Jesus, kid. You have a lot to learn, and I sure as hell don't have a lot of time to teach you."

Ein scowled. "What do you mean?"

Before Teddy could answer, the overhead lights brightened, and the air brakes squealed as the train came to an abrupt stop. Groggy passengers rubbed their eyes, bewildered.

"Remain in your seats!" a voice said over the intercom.

A woman with greasy blonde hair at the front of the train uttered a low whistle. "Look—we're in Vegas!"

Passengers in window seats pressed their faces against the glass, while those in aisle seats leaned over for a peek at the infamous city. Teddy lifted his window's shutter. It had been many years since he last visited Vegas. The skyline was barely recognizable. Pillars of black smoke rose from the Mandarin Oriental Hotel. The Bellagio Tower was reduced to steel beams and rubble. Individual fires dotted the streets as far as he could see. Tattered tarps bearing biohazard symbols covered many low-rise buildings. The Palms Palace Hotel had plastic wrapped around it, and The STRAT had toppled. At the Palazzo, sheets hung from shattered windows had been redecorated with pleas for help. Abandoned vehicles clogged the freeways. The dead lay rotting on the asphalt, and birds leisurely feasted on them. A thin layer of ash and sand covered everything.

Along the train station's platform, people were crammed into makeshift holding pens manned by FEMA officers in riot gear. Those inside the pens pounded their open palms against the chain-link fences and shouted in vain at the train.

A large convention center stood just beyond the train station. Its grimy windows were riddled with bullet holes, and the building's exterior was covered with soot. A faded banner draped from the roof read, *LAS VEGAS REGIONAL FEMA QUARANTINE CENTER*, in bold blue letters.

Teddy turned away from the grim hellscape and focused on the people trapped in the uncovered pens. Judging by the boils and blisters marring their skin, they'd been roasting under the unrelenting desert sun for some time. He saw the fear, anguish, and raw panic on their faces and was sure he'd never forget the sight. He looked away, shaking his head.

Ein stared down at those crying out from the cages as the police stood by and watched. "This isn't right."

"After everything you've seen, are you really surprised?" Teddy said.

"I just hoped that things would get better once we left Tucson."

"If anything, I bet they're only going to get worse."

The doors at the front of the carriage opened, and two FEMA officers brandishing rifles entered. Lieutenant Hock trailed behind them, his hands clasped behind his back and a bushy brow cocked as he studied the passengers.

"Why are these people standing when they were told to remain seated?"

The officers looked flustered until one of them took control. "Everyone—back in your seats! Now!"

While Hock stayed behind and watched, the officers moved down the aisle, using their rifles to shove anyone who hadn't moved fast enough back to their seats.

"Hey!" a middle-aged man shouted. His silver-brown hair was pulled back in a ponytail, and he wore baggy jogging pants and a sleeveless T-shirt. He stepped into the aisle, blocking the officers, and pointed out the windows. "What they're doing to those people isn't right! They could at least put a tarp over them or something. It's torture to keep them out in the sun like that!"

One officer lunged, driving his knee into the man's abdomen and simultaneously slamming the butt of his rifle against his head. The man went down, and a woman at the back of the carriage screamed.

The other officer glared at her. "Quiet down!"

Both officers delivered a volley of kicks to the man's frail body. The woman at the back wept, burying her face against her husband's shoulder. He held her close, his own face contorted with fear. The other passengers watched in horror, silent and frozen in their seats.

Teddy reached over and banded his arm across Ein to hold him back as he tried to stand, his fists clenched. He tried to dislodge him, but Teddy shook his head and tightened his grip. With his back pressed against the seat, Ein glared down at the floor, his entire body shaking.

He may be green, but at least he has heart.

The officers continued to kick and stomp even after the man was unconscious, and blood poured from his nose and mouth.

"Enough," Hock said. "Get him back in his seat."

The officers grabbed the limp body and shoved him into his seat, but he slumped to the floor.

"Does anybody else wish to voice their concerns?" Hock asked. The passengers remained quiet. Hock glanced out the window and noticed the commotion on the platform. "Good. Officers cover the windows. Nobody else needs to get all worked up."

The officers slung their rifles over their shoulders and marched down the aisle, pulling down shutters.

"There was a disturbance inside the convention center, so some of the more disruptive individuals had to be isolated outside. Everything is under control now," Hock explained to the frightened passengers before gesturing at the platform. "They'll be accompanying us from here on out."

Teddy reached up and closed his window shutter as an officer approached. The officer leveled him with an icy glare, but moved on to the next row.

"Where, exactly, are we all headed?" Teddy asked. "I didn't see Vegas on the itinerary."

"All will be revealed in due course," Hock said as he strolled down the aisle, giving Teddy a meaningful glance before following the officers into the next carriage. "In the meantime, sit back and make room."

There was a loud hiss as the train's main doors unfolded. A few minutes later, eight FEMA officers led a line of bedraggled men and women aboard the locomotive. The officers carried fiberglass batons and wore helmets with clear visors; black balaclavas obscured the rest of their faces. They'd donned full body armor with protective pads for their arms and legs.

The new arrivals kept their heads down and looked as if they hadn't bathed in days. Heat radiated off their sweaty bodies. Their blistered skin was bright red, and pus oozed from open sores. Strips of dry, dead skin hung from their arms and faces. Many were covered in bruises and struggled to walk.

"Take the first open seat you see!" one of the escorting officers shouted. "Hurry up!"

The officers shoved anyone who hesitated into the few remaining seats and jabbed weary people's ribs with their batons to keep them moving. Teddy kept a watchful eye on the new officers as they barked orders. A few clearly had some prior law enforcement experience; they were quieter, calmer, and stayed in the background.

The others looked like ordinary survivors who had been given uniforms and guns because they were the few who remained able to carry out these duties. Even if Homeland Security had augmented the military and the local agencies, Teddy knew there couldn't be enough first responders left alive to fill an entire national FEMA battalion, so it was the only explanation that made sense. These officers were exceptionally jumpy, reminding Teddy of rookie guards from his prison days.

Almost everyone had taken their seats, and the remaining few were being escorted to the back door of the carriage. One officer stopped at Teddy's row and glared at him with beady brown eyes. He was attempting to look intimidating, but it took everything in Teddy to smother a laugh. The man's riot helmet was askew, and pimples covered his portly cheeks. A single bead of sweat clung to the tip of his red, bulbous nose. A black balaclava covered his mouth. Considering how dangerous fear could be, especially when it was combined with inexperience, Teddy found it surprising that Homeland Security wasn't being a little choosier about its recruits. Or maybe the higher-ups just didn't care anymore.

"What are you looking at, punk?" The chubby FEMA officer clenched his baton. "Eyes forward!"

Teddy turned and fixed his eyes on the headrest in front of him. Satisfied, the officer snorted and walked away.

"Jesus, could you stop bringing us unwanted attention?" Ein whispered, keeping his eyes down as he wiped sweat off his forehead and sighed. "What is it with you and cops?"

Teddy glanced at Ein. "I don't know who these people are, but most of them weren't anything remotely close to cops before the virus struck."

A few minutes after the officers escorted the stragglers into the next carriage, the air brakes disengaged, and the train crept forward. Teddy heard the shouts of the people on the platform outside. It sounded like a lot of them were still in the pens, crying and begging for help. The din faded as the train gained momentum, leaving what remained of Las Vegas behind.

Teddy leaned back against the headrest, but Ein leaned forward, nervously glancing over his shoulder and digging his nails into his armrests.

"Relax," Teddy said. "You're shaking the whole damn train."

Ein scoffed. "Well, I'm sure glad you're comfortable, but when we left Tucson, you acted like you were ready to lead a revolution! Now you're telling me to relax like we're on vacation! Remember what you told me? There are more of us than there are of them."

"I haven't slept for days, kid," Teddy muttered. "Get off my ass."

"So, all that was just talk." Ein's voice was heavy with disappointment. "You know, I believed you. Now I see you're just like the others back at the stadium who talked a bunch of shit but did nothing. You're—"

Teddy reached over and snatched Ein's shirt collar, yanking him close. Ein's eyes grew wide, and the other passengers nearby pretended not to notice their confrontation.

"Listen, you damn kid!" Teddy brought their faces close together and hissed, "If you want to survive, you've got to learn how to pick your battles! We don't know what we're headed toward or what kind of support we'll have when we get there, but you're ready to go all-in against a bunch of trigger-happy thugs?"

"I was just saying that maybe we—"

"I can't tell you how many times I've seen punks' skulls get smashed just because they've got chips on their shoulders and something to prove!"

Ein held up his trembling hands. "I-I'm sorry. I didn't—"

"Shut up and figure out the lay of the land before you do something stupid and get us both killed. Got it?"

Ein nodded, his face pale just as the rear door opened and an armed FEMA officer walked down the aisle on patrol. Teddy let go of Ein's shirt before he reached their row, and they kept quiet as the officer passed and disappeared through the front door.

As soon as he was out of earshot, Ein cleared his throat and whispered, "I want to survive this. I also want to help you. What these people are doing isn't right."

"Then you need to listen to what I say." Teddy said without looking at him head-on. "It's going to take us a while, but we'll figure it all out. My old ass has been around long enough to learn a few things." He paused and yawned. "Once we get to where we're going, we can plan our next step. Sound good?"

"Yeah," Ein said, scratching the back of his neck, "but what do I do in the meantime?"

"I already told you," Teddy mumbled. "Relax. Go to sleep."

"Teddy?"

"Yeah?"

"I don't want to die in some cage."

An image of Jane and Danny flashed in Teddy's mind; the haunting visage of their dying faces was etched into his memory. His pigheaded plan to get to the stadium led to their deaths, and Teddy had vowed never to make that mistake again. He fixed Ein with a sober look.

"Kid, I promise you that no matter what, I'm getting us out of this new place—wherever it is."

"I appreciate that," Ein said with a wan smile. He paused as if to weigh his words before he added, "If you think I'll slow you down, though, you can go on your own. You don't owe me anything."

"No, I don't, but I owe them everything," Teddy quickly answered.

"Who?" Ein asked, confused.

Teddy sniffed, closed his eyes, and leaned his head back. "I'll get us out of here. Just be patient."

They sat in silence as the train chugged on. Teddy slipped into an uneasy slumber, in which he swore he once again held Danny's stiff corpse in his arms.

2

NOVEMBER 24th

The full moon illuminated overgrown cornfields that stretched for miles. Glistening ice crystals covered the stalks; a thin layer of frost blanketed everything.

Teddy stared dispassionately out the window as the train barreled onward. As exhausted as he was, proper sleep remained elusive—his unsteady mind made sure of that.

The train rounded a bend in the tracks, and Teddy glimpsed a glowing compound far off in the distance. Whatever it was, the train was headed right for it.

He sat up and checked on the other passengers. Most appeared to be on edge and struggling with the same sleeplessness that plagued him. Hell, he couldn't blame them.

Ein sat with his arms wrapped around his stomach, a sour expression on his face. Over the last few hours, the dark circles under his eyes had deepened.

The air brakes squealed; the sound reverberating through the carriage as the train slowed to a crawl. As the other passengers looked around and opened their window shutters, they realized no one could see beyond the towering, frozen stalks of corn.

Bright white light shone through the windows as the train passed through a chain-link fence topped with razor wire and came to a stop. Spotlights surrounded the area. The FEMA banner had fallen off the fence, exposing a faded sign beneath it: *United States Customs and Border Protection—Region VII Detention Center.*

Overhead, nozzles spritzed the train with blue disinfectant. The murky substance obscured the view through the windows, prompting the passengers to focus on the carriage doors. Nervous chatter and confused murmurs filled the air.

"Are we at another quarantine center?" Ein asked.

"No, kid. I think this is something different," Teddy said.

The front door of the carriage slid open and four police officers entered, each carrying a baton. They wore long, black peacoats, tactical pants, leather gloves, and calf-length jackboots. Their jackets bore FEMA insignias, but no nametags or other badges. Black balaclavas left only their eyes visible.

"Everyone, up!" one of them shouted, his voice muffled by the balaclava. "Make your way to the front and head out in an orderly fashion!"

The officers started pulling passengers out of their seats by their collars and shoving them down the aisle toward the door. "Move! Now!"

A woman at the back cried, and some men grew vocal in their protests, but the officers ignored them and continued to prod them along like cattle. Teddy and Ein stepped out of their row and hurried down the aisle with the others. The air outside was bitterly cold and damp. Searchlights from a nearby watchtower bathed the area in harsh light as they scanned the group emerging from the train. Chemical foggers spewed a white haze, adding to the surreal atmosphere. Teddy's breath escaped in small puffs of condensation as he crossed his arms over his chest. Ein cupped his hands over his mouth to keep them warm.

They led the group through a long, narrow corridor made of chain-link fencing to a windowless building with a gigantic television screen mounted above the door. A biting breeze whistled by, making the group shiver as they shuffled forward.

FEMA officers with mirrored visors and heavy winter coats stood on both sides of the corridor, their assault rifles held at the ready to shoot at the first sign of unrest. The television by the door flickered to life, displaying the image of a well-dressed man with the Department of Homeland Security's emblem on the wall behind him.

"Welcome!" he said with a tight smile. "My name is Mark Hammond; I'm your camp administrator. It is my great pleasure to welcome you to our facility. It is our goal to help fulfill the agency's critical mission: repair national infrastructure, clean and rebuild our cities, and repopulate this great country. I understand this task may not be one that you have chosen, but I assure you that your work is vital to the survival of our nation. Future generations will benefit from what you do here, and all of you will be remembered as heroes, not just survivors. The able-bodied will be expected to contribute, and will be assigned appropriate work details. No matter your trade or level of education, we will find the right job for you. In exchange, we will provide you with safety, hot meals, medical care, and humane, comfortable living quarters. You will not have to forage for your next meal, search for clean water, or fight just to survive. Here, you are safe. However, those who choose civil disobedience or to commit criminal acts will face severe consequences. If we don't all work together, this will fall apart. As you step through the door, you will begin your repatriation process and become part of a new world—a better world. I look forward to working with you, and I thank you for your contribution to this noble cause."

The screen blinked, and the recorded message began again as people continued to trickle from the train and walk down the corridor. "Welcome! My name is Mark Hammond; I'm your camp administrator. It is my great pleasure to welcome you to our facility. It is our goal—"

Teddy passed through the doorway and entered a long, windowless room with multiple stalls lining the walls. None of them had doors, just moldy shower curtains. Gymnasium lights dangled from the ceiling, and air ducts were suspended from the exposed steel rafters. The biting cold outside gave way to a musky heat generated by too many bodies and the overworked bulbs in the gymnasium.

People from the train wandered the room, confused and frightened, talking over each other, unsure of what to do. A handful of FEMA officers barked orders from the middle of the room. They looked just as frightened and confused as the passengers, and formed a circle as more people streamed in, shouting questions at them.

"What a clusterfuck," Teddy said to Ein, who stood close by.

The officers became more and more anxious as the crowd swarmed them, outnumbering them. One officer with a sergeant's insignias lowered his balaclava and brought a megaphone to his lips. After clearing his throat and keying the mic, he said, "This is Sergeant Mayville speaking! Everyone stop talking and make your way to one of the stalls! A medical staff member will—"

A man frantically scanning the crowd interrupted him. "Where's my wife? We were together at the station, but now I can't find her!"

Others followed suit and began shouting over each other. Some officers pulled out their batons, standing in defensive positions as the crowd grew more agitated.

Mayville continued as if there'd been no disruption. "A medical staff member will be with you shortly. You need to—" Even amplified by the megaphone, the crowd soon drowned his voice out, so Mayville cleared his throat again and turned the volume up. "You need to find an open stall and enter it right now!"

The man searching for his wife pushed between two officers even as they tried to push him back with their batons. "I'm not going anywhere without Mary!"

Mayville pulled out his pistol and fired at the ceiling. People screamed and ducked. Teddy crouched down with Ein, but Mayville kept his smoking pistol pointed at the ceiling, gritting his teeth as he glared at the crowd. A trickle of plaster dust fluttered down from the rafters and landed on his head, but the crowd remained silent.

"Shut up and stay back, or I'll shoot!" Beads of sweat rolled down Mayville's forehead. He waved his pistol toward the crowd. "Move! Now! One person per stall!"

In a quick and hushed manner, the crowd dispersed and headed toward the stalls, bumping and tripping over each other as they went. The officers spread out, brandishing their batons and shouting at their charges to hurry.

"See you in a bit," Teddy told Ein. "Don't start any shit."

"That goes double for you," Ein said.

They split up and moved toward some of the last remaining stalls on opposite sides of the room.

"Hurry! Get in there!" a young female officer told Teddy, pointing her baton at one of the empty stalls.

Teddy frowned and stepped into the small concrete space. He turned around, but couldn't see which one Ein had taken.

Mayville relaxed, wiped sweat off his brow, and holstered his pistol before pulling his balaclava back up over his nose and mouth. "Remain in your stall until medical screens you! Do not talk to anyone else!"

FEMA officers walked along both sides of the room, pulling the curtains closed on each of the stalls. Teddy glared at a short, fat officer as he passed by his stall. The officer glared back and jerked the curtain shut. Teddy sighed and sat against the wall, his feet spread out in front of him. With the cold concrete pressed against the back of his head, he stared at the ceiling. He wasn't certain what he had walked into, but it felt uncannily like his processing at USP Tucson so many years ago. He closed his eyes and waited.

After a few minutes, he heard muffled screams and the unmistakable sounds of people being knocked around. The chatter on the officers' Motorola radios intensified, filling the air with static and fragmented commands. Teddy jumped to his feet and clenched his fists in case he needed to defend himself. He narrowed his eyes at the closed curtain; whatever was happening out there didn't sound like a routine medical screening.

Ten minutes passed; then more than an hour ticked away. The screaming eventually stopped, but Teddy didn't let his guard down and didn't take his eyes off the curtain.

Finally, it opened. Teddy's heart raced as adrenaline coursed through his veins. He was ready.

Much to his surprise, there were no officers prepared to apprehend him—only a tall man with untidy black hair and misaligned glasses. The man's silver name tag identified him as Dr. Demarest. A young, black woman in blue scrubs and a mask followed the doctor and pushed through a rolling kiosk that held a computer and a tray containing several numbered syringes.

"What happened out there?" Teddy asked, craning his neck to look over the doctor's shoulders.

"Nothing," Demarest replied. "Hold out your wristband."

"What was all the screaming about?" Teddy persisted.

"Show the nurse your barcode."

Teddy looked down at the wristband he had received at the stadium. It was faded, stained, and fraying, but the barcode was still readable. The nurse took a handheld scanner off the cart and Teddy extended his arm. After scanning the barcode, the nurse turned her attention to the computer on the cart and read out what appeared on the screen.

"His name is Teddy Sanders, and he's from the Tucson, Arizona, center. H7N9 antigens were detected in his blood test. Sugar levels, kidney and liver function, and electrolytes came back normal. The potassium level was slightly low, but within normal range. CBC is normal. Cholesterol panel is normal. No STDs." She paused. "They don't need this one. They haven't flagged his chart."

"Flagged?" Teddy asked. "What the hell does that mean?"

Demarest ignored his question and took a penlight from his pocket, then shone the beam at Teddy's pupils. Teddy squinted and turned away from the blinding light.

"The test conducted in Tucson says that you have H7N9 antigens in your system. How long ago did you have the flu?" he asked, shining the light in Teddy's ear.

"I don't know," Teddy muttered. "A few weeks ago, I suppose. I lost track of time for a while there."

"You recovered without incident?"

"I'm standing here, aren't I?"

Demarest grabbed Teddy's chin, turning his head in the opposite direction. "Are you currently on any prescription medication?" he asked, shining the light in Teddy's other ear.

"No."

"Any chronic diseases or handicaps?"

"No."

"Do you take illicit drugs?"

"Why? Do you have any?" Teddy asked with a sly grin.

"Yes or no, Mr. Sanders," Demarest said with a sigh.

"No, I don't take any of that shit."

"Cancer? Heart problems?"

"None that I'm aware of."

Demarest turned Teddy's head toward him and ordered, "Open."

Teddy opened his mouth as the doctor peered down his throat for a few seconds. After letting go of Teddy's chin, the doctor turned off the penlight and returned it to his pocket. Nothing in his demeanor indicated whether he had found what he was looking for until he spoke to the nurse instead of Teddy.

"He's healthy and cleared for high-risk work duties because of his H7N9 immunity. No work restrictions. You may proceed." Demarest yawned and exited the stall.

The nurse pushed her cart toward Teddy and typed something on the computer's keyboard.

"Hold out your wristband again," she said without looking away from the screen.

Teddy extended his arm once more. She cut off the wristband and picked up a syringe from the tray, scanned the barcode taped to it, and typed some more. Teddy started to lower his arm.

"No, keep it extended; turn your hand toward the ceiling and make a fist."

"Why?"

"I need to give you an injection."

"What's in it?" he asked, suspicion creeping into his voice.

The nurse sighed. "Honey, do I need to get the officer, or are you going to do as you're told?"

With a sigh of his own, Teddy brought his arm back up, turned it, and made a fist. The nurse grabbed his wrist and stuck the needle into his forearm.

"This is a tracking chip; it'll serve as your identification at the camp." As she injected a small, metallic device under his skin, she added, "Along with storing your medical records and personnel file, this chip will allow you access to different buildings, depending on what clearance level you're granted and whatever job you're assigned."

She dropped the used needle into a small red bin on the bottom tier of her cart. Teddy frowned at the small knot protruding from his forearm. The foreign object was cold and irritated his skin.

"It itches."

"Don't scratch it," the nurse said. "The swelling should go down in a day or so. Soon, you'll forget it's even there. Questions?"

"Plenty, but something tells me I'd get more answers from a brick wall."

"You'd do well to remember your place here," she warned. "We all have jobs here; I'm just doing mine. You can step out and join the others now. You're done."

The nurse pushed her cart over to the next stall, where the doctor was waiting. Scratching his arm, Teddy exited the stall and studied the main room. Most of the stalls had their curtains pulled back and were empty.

"Medical reminder," what sounded like a recording announced through the overhead speakers. "It is your duty to report any signs of illness or flu-like symptoms. Failure to do so is a punishable offense."

Two doctors and a small group of nurses visited the remaining occupied stalls while FEMA officers watched from the middle of the room. Teddy looked down at the floor. His eyes grew wide, and a chilling sensation shot down his spine when he caught sight of the fresh blood droplets tracing a path across the floor to a door.

"Ein? Are you still in here, kid?" There was no response, so Teddy tried again, a little louder. "Ein! Are you in here?"

Silence.

Teddy jumped when one officer shouted, "Quit standing around and head outside!"

"I'm looking for a friend."

The officer pulled out his baton and waved it in the air, then pointed at the door. "I don't care who you're looking for! If you don't move your ass through that door right now, I'll crack your skull!"

Teddy stuffed his hands into his pockets and marched, following the drops of blood to the door. All he could do was hope the kid was okay, although hope had yet to do him any favors.

Outside, the air was frigid and a brightly lit concrete pad awaited. Squinting, he held up a hand to shield his eyes from the blinding halogen spotlights as he surveyed the complex. Multiple one-story concrete buildings that looked like barracks dotted the landscape for as far as he could see, as well as high-mast lights and guard towers. Most of the buildings were numbered, and many bore US Border Patrol seals. An array of communication antennas and satellite dishes crowned a large concrete tower that stood in the center of the camp; it reminded Teddy of an air traffic control tower. A massive chain-link fence topped with razor wire surrounded the entire camp. Teddy felt dwarfed by the complex's sprawl.

One building stood out from all the others: a five-story structure on a small hill overlooking the camp. It had narrow slits for windows and was painted a drab gray. It had narrow slits for windows and was painted a drab gray, exuding an air of ominous authority. This stark edifice towered over the surrounding single-story barracks, its imposing presence impossible to ignore. The building reminded Teddy of the SHU back at USP Tucson, a place synonymous with isolation and punishment.

Two FEMA officers carrying rifles and wearing full riot gear stood at the corner of the concrete slab, along with a third man in a black trench coat that didn't feature any insignias or rank. He held a small scanner and a tablet with a touch screen. Standing behind them was Hock from the train; his dress uniform and black beret set him apart as the superior officer on the premises.

A small group of people in civilian clothes stood behind the lieutenant, shivering and waiting.

"You!" the man in the trench coat called out to Teddy. "Step forward!"

Teddy did as he was told, and the man ordered him to hold out his chip. Teddy held his arm out, waiting as the man's fingers clumsily poked and prodded the tablet's screen. Hock stared at Teddy, who averted his gaze to avoid eye contact. After a few seconds, Hock's face lit up with recognition.

"Weren't you the one who gave my officers a hard time on the train?" A slow grin formed on his face, even though Teddy kept quiet. "Ah, yes. I remember. Teddy Sanders, right?"

"I don't remember your name," Teddy said, looking the lieutenant in the eyes.

"Lieutenant Hock—I'm in charge of this camp's security. I told you back on the train that we'd be seeing a lot of each other, didn't I?"

"Would say it's an honor, but you don't seem like the type of moron who would buy that bullshit," Teddy said.

Both FEMA officers stepped forward and pointed their rifles at Teddy's chest, while the man in the trench coat just stared at him as if he couldn't believe he had that kind of nerve.

"Show some respect!" one officer barked.

"Stand down," Hock ordered.

Stunned, the officers lowered their weapons and stepped back. The man in the trench coat focused on his tablet again.

Hock kept his sharp gaze on Teddy and nodded. "You're correct, and you don't seem like the type of moron who would sell me such bullshit. Not everyone here appreciates honesty like I do."

"Duly noted," Teddy muttered, arm still extended for the man with the tablet.

He ran the scanner over Teddy's chip. "You can lower your arm now." He hooked the scanner back onto his utility belt. "It will take me a moment to enter you into our system."

Teddy crossed his arms over his chest, shivering in the bitter cold. He looked over his shoulder and noticed a small line forming behind him, but he didn't see Ein.

"Have you seen a kid in his early twenties?" Teddy asked Hock. "Purple hair. Couldn't miss him."

"No, I haven't," Hock replied candidly. "He must still be inside, waiting to be examined."

Instead of making Teddy feel better, the lieutenant's response only made him more apprehensive.

Reading from his tablet, the man in the trench coat said, "We need more people in the kitchen, so I'm assigning you to Sergeant Flood's detail in dorm eighteen."

"Does this guy look like a cook to you?" Hock asked, bemused.

"Sir?"

"He's immune—why waste him? He needs to work the city, not chop carrots."

"Yes, sir," the man said. "I'll place him on the CDT crew in dorm thirty-six: Sergeant Clark's detail."

"CDT?" Teddy asked, giving the man a quizzical look.

Before he could explain, the lieutenant cut in. "Not dorm thirty-six. Clark is a good guy, but he's soft. This one needs someone hard."

"Hard?" the man asked, raising an eyebrow at the lieutenant.

"Put him on Parham's detail in dorm twenty. I think he'll be able to handle him."

"But, sir," the man in the trench coat said. "Sergeant Clark has empty—"

"It wasn't a request," Hock growled. He narrowed his eyes. "Make it happen."

"Yes, sir," the man said, looking back down at his tablet.

"Parham's one of those people I mentioned earlier, Sanders," Hock said. "Someone who doesn't appreciate blunt honesty."

"Why are you putting me with him?" Teddy asked.

Hock smiled as the man in the trench coat finished updating the information in the system.

"It's done." He pointed to the rows of concrete barracks in the distance. "Report to dorm twenty."

Teddy wandered toward a group of civilians huddled on the sidewalk nearby. They were all middle-aged men and wore red armbands. Even though they also wore thick coats, gloves, and knit hats, they looked as if they were freezing. Most appeared malnourished, too; their eyes were sunken, and their cheekbones jutted out unnaturally, giving them the look of emaciated, skeletal ghouls.

As Teddy approached, one scowling man asked, "Which dorm have you been assigned to?"

"Twenty."

The men murmured and shook their heads, and one said, "Sorry to hear that, brother."

A bald, black man wearing a pair of old Timberlands, a gray sweatshirt, and khaki pants said with a hint of a southern drawl, "I was wondering if they'd send me somebody. You must've pissed someone off something fierce."

"I reckon so," Teddy grumbled, glancing over his shoulder toward Hock.

"Well, I'm dorm twenty's ambassador—at least that's what they say." He paused and chuckled. "I'll help get you settled. My name is Rodrick Perry, but I was one of the first to arrive, so folks around here just call me Old Perry. You got a name, new blood?"

"Teddy," he said as his gaze passed over the small crowd, scanning for any sign of purple hair.

"Nice to meet ya, Teddy." Perry turned and started walking, calling over his shoulder, "Let's get you to your new home. Follow me."

Teddy looked wistfully over his shoulder, but Perry had turned in time to catch him in the act and stopped.

"There's nothing for you back there anymore." He pointed at his red armband. "It's past curfew, and you really don't want to loiter without one of these on."

"I'm waiting for someone," Teddy said. "A friend of mine. He came on the train with me."

"You're better off trying to find him in the morning at breakfast. We sure can't stand around out here any longer," Perry warned. "Come on. Let's go."

Teddy stuck his hands in his pockets and trailed Perry down a walkway, examining the squalid surroundings as he went. The narrow pathway wove between multiple jerry-built concrete buildings with flat roofs. The hasty construction was clear even in the moonlight—large cracks branched up from their foundations, and many of the buildings appeared to be sloped, as though they were slowly sinking into the earth. Lime deposits and mold had already formed from the runoff coming from the rooftop HVAC units. None of the buildings had windows, just numbered doors that barely fit in their frames. Teddy was a little surprised at how shoddy they were, given the government's unparalleled expertise at squandering money.

"What gives?" Teddy asked from where he trailed behind Perry.

"What do you mean?" Perry asked.

Teddy's voice dripped with distaste as he replied, "Why is this place such a pile of shit?"

Perry shrugged. "When the virus spread the way it did, they were in a hurry to throw all this together. It used to be an immigration detention facility, but they added more dorms and fences."

"What happened to the detainees?" Teddy asked, even though he was pretty sure he knew the answer.

"I never asked, and they never offered that information."

Mounds of putrefying trash surrounded small alleyways and haphazardly strung clotheslines. Rats and field mice scurried from one alley to another, squeaking and fleeing as the two men walked by. The ripe stench of human feces and urine twisted Teddy's face into an expression of revulsion.

"You get used to the smell, believe it or not," Perry said with another shrug.

"Where the hell does all this trash come from?"

"We're overpopulated, but they keep sending us more folks. The cops had a crew dig a landfill a few miles down the road, but they can't seem to keep up with demand. There was talk about putting some incinerators up near the clinic, but it looks like that was just talk."

"They have a clinic here?" Teddy asked, surprised.

"Sure do, but it's not much. It's over in the administration building: the low-rise on the hill. Did you see it when you came in?"

"Hard to miss it," Teddy said as he stared at a stained blanket flapping on a clothesline. "I can't believe people came here with nothing but the clothes on their backs and still accumulated so much junk."

"They didn't bring any of this stuff on the trains," Perry said. "The vultures pick it up and smuggle it in. Dorms are stuffed to capacity—

some even have folks sleeping on the floor—but that doesn't stop people from wanting little pieces of their old lives to cling to."

Teddy wondered who these vultures were, but he was too tired and cold to press the issue.

Unlike most of the others, building twenty sat level and didn't seem to suffer from too many structural cracks. The door had a small biometric device mounted next to it. Perry placed his forearm against the fob, and the door unlocked.

"Perry, Rodrick—dorm twenty custodian—access granted," a robotic female voice announced from the speaker.

"Use your chip to get in and out of the buildings here," Perry explained, pointing at his arm. He pushed the door open and extended a hand. "I figure you're ready to catch some sleep after that train ride. We'll go over everything else you need to know in the morning."

Teddy brushed past him and stepped inside. The heat was on, but it was still uncomfortably cold. He cupped his hands together and blew on his icy palms. Dim lights dangled from the ceiling between ventilation shafts. The room had bunk beds lining the left and right walls. A row of lockers and wooden benches ran down the center, dividing the space in half. Communal showers and restroom stalls with stainless steel doors took up the back wall. To Teddy's surprise, most of the bunks were empty and had nothing but thin mattresses and wool blankets. He counted six people who were fast asleep—nobody was awake to greet him.

Perry closed the door and joined Teddy. So as not to disturb the others, he whispered, "See? It's not so bad here. At least our dorm isn't overcrowded like the regular crews."

"Why is that?"

"Last month, we lost half the dorm to typhoid or something else— they never really explained what. One worker, Mitch, caught a bug and it spread like wildfire. Our dorm was under quarantine for a week. Everyone who was sick got sent to medical and never came back." Perry leveled Teddy with a stern look. "Our details have the nicest dorms, but our work carries the highest risks. That's the life of a vulture."

"You still haven't explained what it is I'm expected to do," Teddy said. "What makes us vultures?"

"We'll cover all that tomorrow, too. Right now, go pick a bunk and try to sleep. I'll show you the chow hall in the morning." Perry clapped Teddy on the back and shuffled off into the shadows.

Teddy wandered over to a lower bunk near the front of the room, away from the others. It would have to do. He sat down and kicked off his boots. Heaving an exhausted sigh, he lay down on his back and grimaced—the mattress was as hard as plywood.

"And here I thought Tucson's mattresses were horrible," he grumbled to himself.

He wrapped himself in the flimsy blanket and rolled over on his side. Despite his discomfort, his eyelids grew heavy and eventually fluttered closed.

Before he could succumb to sleep, a vision of Jane and Danny flashed across his mind. At first, he saw their smiling faces, but then they morphed into skeletal apparitions.

Teddy's eyes sprang open, and his heart raced. With a heavy sigh, he rolled onto his back and stared up at the empty bunk above him. He had many regrets, but his biggest one was not telling Jane the truth while he still had the chance.

He had begun to fall in love with her, a feeling he rarely let himself acknowledge. If he had just opened up to her, maybe they would never have ended up in that wretched stadium. They could have gone off on their own, escaping the nightmare of Tucson. And if Danny had recovered, maybe Jane wouldn't have gotten sick at all.

But it was too late. They were gone.

The thought of Jane and Danny lying together in some mass grave and covered in slaked lime brought tears to his eyes. He knew it wouldn't do him any good to reminisce, nor would it help him mourn their loss. He had to keep moving forward, as he'd promised he would.

Teddy wiped away the tears and forced his eyes to close. Several hours passed before he slipped into an uneasy slumber.

3

NOVEMBER 25th

Dawn broke, and the first rays of sunlight bounced off the frost covering the vast sea of dead cornstalks. Vibrant shades of bronze, red, and orange lit up the solar panels that powered the camp as darkness dissolved into daylight. Plumes of steam rose from the dormitories' boiler furnaces.

A two-story farmhouse stood a few miles away from the camp; a narrow strip of gravel connected them. With its wraparound porch, white board and batten siding, wood shingles, green storm shutters, and copper weathervane, the house looked like it had been plucked right out of a Norman Rockwell painting. Mark Hammond hated every inch of the place.

Wearing nothing but a bathrobe, he slouched in his office chair, staring with contempt at the camp through his study window. Being isolated and stuck in the middle of the country was not only an unfamiliar way of life but also as far as one could get from the cosmopolitan lifestyle he'd once envisioned for himself. His reassignment packet was on the desk. He hadn't gone over every detail, but he'd read enough to know just how costly his ticket to a Cabinet position was going to be.

"Three years," he muttered as he stared down at the glass of whiskey in his hand. "Three goddamn years."

It felt like a prison sentence. Then again, he figured he deserved it.

As he closed his eyes, he saw Laura lying on the bed, clutching the blanket against her sweaty body. She looked up at him with desperate, teary eyes, her blonde hair spread over the pillow. At the end, even breathing took a painful amount of effort on her part—it had hurt him just to look at her.

Hammond took another swig to drown out her memory. His head swam, and for a moment, he thought he was going to collapse as he waited for the room to stop spinning. Even operating on only two hours of sleep and a diet consisting of little more than fermented grains, he knew his health was failing, but he didn't care. Alcohol was the only thing that offered him a diversion from soul-crushing loneliness and crippling depression. He closed his eyes, but jolted awake as he heard a vehicle approaching.

A military Humvee sped along the road from the direction of the camp. The last thing he wanted was a visitor. Hammond scowled, raised the glass to his cracked lips, and finished his drink in one gulp as the vehicle came to a stop in front of the porch. Soon after, he heard a car door slam and heavy footsteps ascend the wooden stairs. After a few minutes, there was a timid knock on the study door.

"What?" Hammond asked without turning from the window.

Its reflective surface allowed him a view of an agent wearing a black suit cracked the door open and poked his head inside. He had an MP5 submachine gun slung around his shoulder and a gold badge clipped to his belt.

"Lieutenant Hock requests an audience. Should I let him in?"

Hammond waved a bony hand in the air and settled deeper into the chair even as he spun it away from the window. The agent opened the door all the way and stood back. Hock wore his dress uniform, and his appearance reflected his usual meticulous attention to detail. He entered the room with his beret tucked under his arm. The agent left the room and shut the door.

"What can I do for you?" Hammond asked. He stared down at the empty glass and absentmindedly rocked it from side to side.

"Three more trains arrived last night," Hock replied.

"Yes, I'm aware," Hammond said, irritated. "What is your point?"

"We cannot accommodate another increase in population. You need to tell Command we've got no more room for anybody else."

Hammond sighed and considered what he must have looked like to the lieutenant. Skinny, hairy legs poked out of his robe. The portion of his face that was visible through his disheveled mop of hair looked haggard and drawn. Hock, however, didn't appear fazed by his appearance.

"You know damn well that I don't control the train schedule," Hammond grumbled. "They're losing their hold on the quarantine centers in the cities, so they're clearing them out as fast as they can. That means all those people head our way, or somewhere like this camp.”

“Could you at least request additional manpower and ammunition to help handle the influx?”

“That’s not how this works. Cheyenne Command and White Mountain are their priorities, and the rest of us get the scraps. They will not send what they already don’t have enough of.”

Hock furrowed his brow. “Then I’d like permission to use the satellite radio and ask for some help myself. Perhaps if they knew of our precarious situation from a military perspective—”

“You know I can’t allow you to do that.”

“With all due respect, sir, what exactly *can* you do?”

Hammond stared at him with an expressionless face. “Mind your tone, or I’ll show you just how fast your title can be stripped away.”

Hock rubbed his forehead and shook his head. “I apologize, but this is dangerous. I can’t continue running exterior work details with minimal staff.”

Hammond frowned and leaned back in his chair. “You have no choice.” He turned the chair back to the window. “The crews must continue their duties and help make the city habitable again.”

“Then I’m going to need more men.”

“That will not happen. You need to learn how to do more with less, or I’ll find someone who will. Recruit from the camp’s population, if you must. I really don’t care as long as the job gets done.”

“They’re civilians,” Hock growled.

Hammond shrugged. “A body is a body.” The phone on the desk rang, and he gave the lieutenant a dismissive wave. “You’re excused.”

Infuriated, Hock turned and stormed out, letting the door slam behind him. Alone again in the dim room, Hammond let out a deep sigh and stared at the ringing phone on his desk. He picked up the receiver and pressed it against his ear.

“Hammond speaking.”

“Good morning,” a nasally voice answered. “This is Melvin Gatsby from research. How are you doing?”

Hammond didn’t respond. After a few seconds of awkward silence, the caller spoke again.

“Uh, sir? Are you there?”

“I’m here.”

“Oh, okay. Well, um, I wanted to give you a progress report if you have time.”

“Go ahead.”

He cleared his throat. “Sir, as expected, the lymphocyte reaction to introducing foreign—"

Hammond set the receiver on the desk as the man prattled on. "Three years of this shit."

He dropped the glass on the carpet and watched it roll away. Minutes later, when the phone call was finally over, he rose from the chair and pulled the curtains until the room was as dark as his current state of mind before flopping back into his chair and closing his eyes.

Once again, he saw Laura's pallid face, heard her begging him for help that he couldn't provide. Despite the severity of her illness, how weak and frail she had appeared, he vividly remembered how hard she struggled as he held the pillow over her face. He remembered the burning sensation in his arms as her nails dug into his skin. Her muffled cries still echoed in his mind. He recalled how her body went limp after what felt like an eternity.

Hammond lowered his chin to his chest and sobbed in the dark.

4

"Wake up," Perry said as he shook Teddy's shoulder.

Teddy's eyes snapped open as he grabbed Perry by the wrist. He shot up, ready to strike, and twisted Perry's arm. Perry cried out in pain and fell to his knees.

As quickly as he seized it, Teddy released the man's wrist and took in his surroundings, taking frantic shallow breaths as recognition gradually dawned on him.

"Are you crazy or something?" Perry asked, rubbing his wrist as he got to his feet and stumbled back, away from Teddy.

"I'm sorry." Embarrassed, Teddy rubbed his eyes and groaned. "I guess I'm a little jumpy."

"I can see that!" Frowning, Perry pointed at the marks on his wrist and then motioned for Teddy to get up. "Come on, you jumpy motherfucker. You need to hurry and shower before you miss breakfast."

Teddy stood, stretched, and popped his neck. "I don't care about chow. I just want to find Ein."

"Ein? Who's that?"

"He's the one I told you about last night. The one I came in with."

"Oh, yeah." Perry rubbed his chin. "I bet he's in the dining hall. As soon as you're ready, we'll head out."

"Sounds like a plan."

Teddy put on his boots, buttoned his shirt, and trudged toward the showers. His new roommates were already dressed in heavy winter clothes.

The showers reminded Teddy of his old high school athletic department. Dingy, off-white tiles covered the floor and walls, and a row of lime-encrusted showerheads hung from the ceiling. Plastic buckets, bars of soap, and piles of damp towels covered in mildew lined the wall. A plastic sign affixed to the wall read, *HEALTH NOTICE—SHOWER FACILITIES USE RECLAIMED WATER—NOT POTABLE—DO NOT DRINK*. A cockroach crawled out of one of the floor drains and scurried by.

Despite how badly he needed a shower, he figured he'd take his chances and go without for another day. Besides, he was way too preoccupied to think about anything as mundane as personal hygiene.

Turning away from the showers, he rounded the corner and discovered a long, steel washbasin mounted under a dirty mirror. A row of faucets poised above the basin, ready to drip water, and a sign on the mirror caught his attention. It read, "Help prevent the spread of infection - wash hands after using the toilet."

He approached the mirror and stared at his reflection, noting his scraggly beard and greasy hair. Several days' worth of dirt was caked in his pores, and his eyes had black bags under them. It didn't matter. He didn't have anybody left to impress.

Running his index finger under the tap, he vigorously rubbed it over his teeth. He didn't know which tasted worse: the water or the grime on his skin. He stuck his mouth under the tap, took a big gulp of water, swished, and spat into the basin.

Back outside, he noticed everyone except for Perry had left.

"That was a fast shower," Perry said.

"Decided against it."

"Probably for the best, since you're already running late."

"I figured," Teddy said, gesturing around the empty dorm to illustrate his point.

"Sorry I didn't wake you sooner. I overslept." Perry paused, frowning. "You really don't want to be late and attract Sergeant Parham's attention. He's ex-military and an asshole, if you ask me."

"Yeah—tell me about it." Teddy looked around at the empty bunks. "But is he really capable of keeping an entire dorm spooked?"

"Yeah," Perry said, rubbing his neck. "He's a petty man, and those are the most dangerous. You'll have to fall in line if you want to survive here."

"Survive? I don't even want to *be* here. I sure as hell didn't ask to be on some sleazeball detail."

"You either pissed somebody off, or you just have rotten luck. I haven't figured out which one yet."

"It was that damned lieutenant who put me here." Teddy frowned as he tried to recall his name. "Lieutenant Hawk or something."

"Hock," Perry said. "At least now I know who you pissed off."

"Christ, Perry, I don't even know what this detail does."

"I'll explain over breakfast. Are you ready? Actually, hold on. I got you something," Perry said as he walked over to his bed and then tossed a khaki jacket to him. "Grabbed this out of my stash. I hope it fits. Had to guess your size. I'll have some hygiene items and more clothes on your bed by tonight so you can take a proper shower."

"Thanks," Teddy said as he zipped it up. "It actually fits pretty well."

"Good—I guess I'm getting good at guessing," he said, adjusting his red armband over his sleeve. "The dorm locks disengage when curfew is over, so you don't need to use your chip to get in and out during the day."

Perry pushed the door open. An icy breeze whistled in through the doorway, and morning sunlight inundated the dim quarters. Perry zipped up his jacket and covered his head with an orange knit cap.

"You coming?" he asked as he held the door open for Teddy.

Bundled-up people crowded the sidewalk between the dorms, shuffling past one another with their eyes on the ground. Others huddled under crude, makeshift shelters in alleyways, taking shelter from the wind. Two officers decked out in full riot gear and helmets with gas masks jostled their way through with their batons.

Teddy noticed right away just how outnumbered the officers were. People glared at them, and some spat on the ground at their heels as they walked away. A few even muttered obscenities at their backs. The officers didn't seem to pay the people any attention as they pushed their way through the crowd.

Teddy kept his back against the doorframe and watched. Children laughed and ran between people's legs while their haggard mothers yelled and chased after them. A group of teenagers sat around a small barrel fire, strumming a country song on an old, beaten-up guitar while a couple of young, giggling girls sat cross-legged in front of them as their eager audience. Groups of men and women engaged in conversation as they walked; couples strolled down the footpath, holding hands as if on a leisurely morning jaunt through a park.

Perry stood next to Teddy and gestured out at the crowd. "See? It's not so bad here."

A few passing by gave Perry the same type of dirty look they gave the officers, but he pretended not to notice.

"Where are we, anyway?" Teddy asked, curious.

"Kansas," Perry said with a chuckle. "We're about fifty miles west of Wichita."

Teddy felt bewildered; he couldn't believe that they had taken him all the way from Arizona to Kansas. "Is it always this crowded?"

"It's getting worse," Perry admitted.

"Finding Ein is going to be tougher than I expected."

A man brushed past Teddy and bumped hard into his chest with his elbow. Teddy stumbled back and caught himself against the wall. The man hurried away without even attempting an apology.

"Hey, asshole! Watch where you're going!"

Teddy balled up his fist and stepped forward, ready to chase after him, but Perry put a hand on his shoulder to hold him in place. People nearby stopped mid-conversation and hurried away, while the teens playing the guitar stopped and looked over at him.

"Don't start a fight outside!" Perry warned. "It's not worth it."

"Why not?" Teddy growled, pointing at the officers with their backs turned. "The cops don't seem too worried about much of anything."

"The ones on the ground aren't who you have to worry about." Perry pointed up at the concrete watchtower in the center of the camp. "If you make a scene and someone up in the control center sees, they'll send a team to scoop you up before you can blink."

Teddy looked up at the tower's mirrored windows and scowled. "Whatever. That prick wasn't worth it."

Disappointed, the teens went back to their music while everyone else resumed their conversations.

"You can't go around starting trouble," Perry said. "This isn't that kind of place."

"Thanks, Dad," Teddy said.

"Attention," a female voice announced over the PA system. "The dining facility will close in fifteen minutes."

"Come on, we have to hurry," Perry said as he started walking ahead. "I'll give you the lay of the land as we go."

Teddy followed Perry through the crowd with his hands in his jacket pockets.

"These buildings we're passing are all other dorms. We're not supposed to go inside. Got it?"

"Uh-huh," Teddy muttered disinterestedly as he stared at the passing faces.

"Oh! Then there's the nightly curfew. It's simple, but—"

"Uh-huh."

Perry didn't stop talking as he pointed out different buildings and waved toward different sections of the camp. Teddy didn't hear a word he said—he was preoccupied with finding Ein. Very few people he passed made eye contact with him, and nobody bothered to exchange the usual bullshit pleasantries.

People had set up makeshift stalls in the alleyways between dorms and along the footpath. Shopkeepers shouted and haggled with customers as they bartered for payment for old clothes, weathered books, and raggedy shoes. Old men sat on crates and smoked stale cigarettes while playing checkers and backgammon. A couple of elderly women were beating rugs strung up on a clothesline with sticks, and children chased around mangy dogs. It surprised Teddy just how much of a community was springing up, but of all the different people he passed, he didn't see anybody who even resembled Ein.

Perry stopped walking and turned to Teddy with his arms crossed. "Are you even listening to me?"

Teddy froze as soon as he looked over and saw the frustration on Perry's face. "No, not really."

"This is important!" Perry protested. "This is your orientation!"

"No offense, but I really don't care," Teddy said, holding his hands up. "All I'm interested in is finding Ein and getting out of here. You can even come with us."

Perry chuckled, shook his head, and kept walking.

"Something funny?" Teddy asked as he followed him. "I was planning on—"

A boy zoomed around his legs while a little girl chased after him, cutting his sentence short. Teddy stumbled and almost tripped.

"I know exactly what you're planning. Do you think you're the first one?" Perry asked, without turning around or acknowledging the kids. "Don't you think others have tried abandoning their work detail as soon as they got on the other side of the fence?"

"Why does that matter?"

"I can show you better than I can tell you."

Perry grabbed Teddy by the wrist and led him down the sidewalk as fast as he could, pushing their way through the morning rush. Teddy could barely keep up, and his wrist started aching from how hard it was being squeezed. He tried to pull his arm free, but Old Perry was deceptively strong.

Around the barracks was a massive concrete courtyard. A murder of crows startled and took flight, cawing as they retreated to higher ground. Unlike the footpaths, the courtyard was hauntingly empty and silent as the grave.

Perry let go of his arm and pointed ahead. Teddy's jaw fell as his gaze focused on the structure in the middle of the space.

Corpses with burlap sacks covering their heads dangled high above the platform housing wooden gallows. The bodies were in various stages of decomposition and had been badly mutilated by hungry wildlife. Crows with dry blood caked on their beaks perched atop the gallows, their feathers ruffled as they stared down at Teddy with their beady, black eyes.

"Jesus Christ…" Teddy muttered as he studied the placards hanging around each corpse's neck in horror.

Sedition.

Murder.

Terrorism.

Rape.

Larceny.

Teddy noticed a few FEMA officers strung up with the same word written on their signs: mutineer. He stepped closer, unaware of the red line painted around the perimeter of the platform. Two officers bundled up in peacoats and black wool balaclavas stood beside the platform, carrying rifles, and eyed the red line as Teddy inched closer to it.

Perry walked up behind Teddy and placed a friendly but restraining hand on his shoulder. "Careful. If you cross that red line, it gives them an excuse to put you up there with the others."

Teddy stopped and stared up at the stiff corpses dangling in the chilly breeze. "There are so many."

"It's an effective scare tactic. Every day you pass by and see new people strung up. Fear keeps order, and order keeps the peace. All that talk you spouted about running away will only lead you up there. They'll call you a terrorist, or claim you committed an act of sedition, but it would end the same way," Perry said. "Then there are those they slay beyond the walls. In a sense, they're lucky. They eat a bullet, but never get turned into a public spectacle." He forced a wan smile as his tone lifted. "But if you keep your head down and mind your own business, you can have a pleasant life here—just like me."

Teddy said nothing as he carefully searched the dead for a familiar form.

"Do you see your friend?" Perry asked.

"No, I don't think so," Teddy said. "It's hard to tell with their heads covered, but I don't think he's there."

"Good."

"Both of you need to move along!" one officer ordered.

"Come on," Perry said as he led him away. "Let's check out the dining hall."

They walked toward a long gymnasium-sized building on the other side of the courtyard. Posters papered the building's walls. One of them showed a smiling man in a FEMA officer's uniform and holding a child. The caption read, *Here to help you.* Someone vandalized one poster with a black Sharpie; *don't believe their lies* scribbled sloppily across it. Two civilians wearing red armbands attempted to peel the poster off the wall while an armed officer supervised.

"What's up with that?" Teddy asked as he stared at the poster.

"Just the work of opportunistic thugs pretending to be freedom fighters," Perry explained with disgust clear in his tone. "Aside from art projects like this one, they're not much of a headache here in the camp, but they can cause real trouble in the city."

"They seem to be making some type of impression, whoever they are," Teddy said.

"Their leaders have silver tongues. Fences can't stop charismatic whispering, I guess." Perry shrugged. "The fact is that we're doing well in here, while folks out there suffer just to survive."

Teddy looked over his shoulder at the distant gallows. "If you call this doing well, more power to you."

People headed toward the dining facility's double doors; a small group of officers stood watch nearby. A middle-aged man and his wife exited and approached Teddy and Perry, glaring at Perry's red armband.

"Fucking collaborator!" the man hocked up a wad of yellow phlegm and spat it at Perry.

Perry froze and watched as it ran down the front of his jacket.

"Charley! Don't!" the woman said as she grabbed the man by his shoulders and pushed him away from Perry. She looked over her shoulder at the officers at the entrance. "Let's go before he calls his friends."

"He'll burn with the rest of them!" the man said ominously as the woman led him away. "Wait and see!"

The couple vanished into the crowd while Perry stood motionless, transfixed by the mess on his jacket.

"You're just going to let him disrespect you like that?" Teddy asked.

Perry took an old handkerchief out of his pocket and cleaned up the phlegm as best as he could. "People feel frustrated." He tucked the handkerchief away. "I'm a target because of my armband. If someone did that to a cop, they'd be beaten—or worse. If they do it to one of us and the cops don't see, nothing happens."

"I don't understand the significance of the armband," Teddy said.

"They're what dorm custodians wear," Perry said as he started walking toward the dining hall again. "We watch after the dorm, clean up, lead orientations: things like that. We help keep the peace as best we can. The cops have a certain level of trust in us, so, naturally, people think we're snitches."

"Are you?" Teddy asked as he followed him.

"Am I what?"

"A snitch."

Perry chuckled. "No, I don't see nothing, and I don't know nothing. I'm happy enough watching over the dorm, but a lot of the others don't share my opinions. Some orderlies think that they're an honorary officer and give the rest of us a bad name."

"I couldn't stay here and play house. I'd escape the first chance I got rather than get stuck cleaning toilets."

"Orderly work isn't for everybody. I suffered enough outside, so I'm not in a hurry to go back out there." Perry pushed open the building's double doors and stepped inside, sniffing the air. "Smells like cabbage soup again. I was hoping they'd make some morning hash."

As soon as Teddy stepped inside, a strong, lingering odor of rotten eggs overpowered him. He grimaced and covered his nose. Around him, throngs of people filled multiple rows of tables that took up most of the windowless room. Fluorescent tubes dangled from the ceiling, and an American flag hung proudly on the wall next to the Department of Homeland Security's flag. Faded posters displaying happy families were plastered under them. Cooks wearing yellow jumpsuits and hairnets manned a serving station. Children ran and played between the tables, while their parents hastily ate what they could. A few groups huddled around their tables far away from the others and engaged in hushed, fervent discussion. A handful of men and women wearing red armbands walked between the tables, eavesdropping. Three officers in riot gear stood in the far corner of the room with their rifles across their chests as they stared uneasily out at the crowd.

To Teddy, the setup was hauntingly familiar.

"Community safety reminder," a recording said over the dining hall's PA system. "If you see or hear anything suspicious, report it to the nearest law enforcement officer or dormitory orderly."

Perry walked past Teddy and headed toward the serving line.

"Do we have seating assignments or anything?" Teddy noticed all the races were mixed—something he never saw back at USP Tucson.

Perry gave him an incredulous look. "No. I'm not sure what you're used to, but it's really not that bad here once you get used to the routine."

"I'm familiar with routines, trust me," Teddy said.

Perry gave him another quizzical look, but kept walking. Teddy carefully looked at the faces gathered around the tables, but he didn't see Ein anywhere.

They grabbed plastic trays and waited in line as the cooks hurriedly ladled out bowls of overcooked cabbage soup. A heavyset man with hairy arms grunted and practically hurled a bowl of soup onto the trays, and the man at the end placed a plastic cup of off-color water next to the bowls. An officer stood behind the serving line and watched the entire operation to ensure it ran smoothly.

Perry walked toward the first open pair of seats he spotted, and Teddy followed. He glanced down at the brown water on his tray and frowned.

"This looks worse than what was in the bathroom," he grumbled.

Perry chuckled and sat. "It's discolored because they treat it with iodine. Safe to drink—don't worry."

He picked up his bowl and sipped his bland soup. Teddy scanned the room with unease.

"Do you see your friend?" Perry asked.

"No, I don't..."

"Maybe you'll have better luck at dinner. We're at the end of breakfast, so he's probably already come and gone."

"It's hard to see much of anything with so many people in here."

"The dining hall closes in five minutes," the woman announced over the PA system. "Please finish your meal and bus your tray. Work call will begin soon."

As if on cue, people started getting up with their trays and walking toward the exit. Parents grabbed their kids by their arms and pulled them to the doors despite their protests and insistence that they be allowed to stay behind and play with their friends.

"You don't have much time, so hurry if you're going to eat," Perry stressed.

Teddy took a sip of the water and grimaced, then pushed the cup aside.

"You get used to the taste," Perry said. He took a greedy drink. "The city's water treatment plant is back up and running. Hopefully, they'll extend a pipeline to us out here in the country."

"That may be so, but in the meantime, I think I'll pass on the water."

Perry grinned and quickly finished his. "A full day of work will change that attitude real fast."

Teddy sipped his soup and gagged at the rancid taste, so he quickly spat it back into his bowl. He set the bowl down, leaned back, and let out a frustrated sigh.

"Well, fuck it. I guess I'm not eating!"

Perry shrugged and slurped down the rest of his soup before he slammed the bowl down with a belch. "The food is hit-or-miss. As of late, it has been getting pretty bland."

Teddy put his elbows on the table, ran his fingers through his hair, and groaned. He could feel his stomach gurgling, and his throat was parched. His body begged him to do what his mind refused to allow him to even ponder.

"You really should eat," Perry said. "Trust me. With your job, you'll need the energy."

"What the hell kind of detail am I on, anyway?" Teddy asked. "What am I getting into?"

"CDT: corpse disposal team." Perry pushed his empty tray aside and leaned over the table. "You collect bodies and disinfect abandoned buildings so another team can clean up and make things habitable again."

"That sounds just fucking wonderful," Teddy said. "So my days are going to consist of carting away dead folks?"

"Dealing with the dead is part of it. That's why they call you vultures. There are other things involved, though, like moving vehicles, but CDT crews are all immune, so you guys get stuck doing the nasty jobs nobody else can do."

"It's funny—I figured surviving the virus was the hardest thing I'd have to do. I thought that the worst was behind me," Teddy said. "The longer I stick around, the more I realize I would've been better off if the damn thing took my life."

"Don't be so glum," Perry said with a forced smile. "You're doing the rest of us a favor, and everyone is grateful. As the city expands, people get moved and given a new life—a second chance."

"What about the immune?" Teddy asked. "Do we get a second chance?"

"Well, I, uh, suppose. Yes, after it's all finished, I assume…" Perry said with no small amount of hesitation. "For now, though, since you can't get the virus again, they keep you working."

"Until?" Teddy prompted him to finish his thought.

Perry shifted in his seat uncomfortably. "I, uh, don't really know when, exactly—"

"Bullshit," Teddy scoffed. "They'll work us until we catch some other fucking disease or drop dead from exhaustion."

"That's, uh, well, not exactly—"

"And there are other risks, right?" Teddy asked. "I'm sure not everyone who survived is holding hands and waiting for Uncle Sam to come save them. Do you think they'll welcome us with open arms?"

"I—I really don't see why they wouldn't," Perry said.

"It's anarchy out there! I bet most folks on this team end up catching a bullet."

"Some officers ride with you to provide security," Perry explained with another fake smile.

"How many?"

Perry lost his smile and scratched the back of his neck. "Not enough. There aren't a lot of officers to go around."

"In other words, those of us who had the virus or are naturally immune are expendable assets."

"Yeah, but valuable ones, if that makes any difference."

"It doesn't, Perry. It really doesn't."

"I wish I had better news for you, but that's just the way things are. I know it sounds harsh, but you have to believe me when I say that things aren't so bad." He spread his arms and gestured around the room. "They're really building something here—a community."

"No, Perry. They built a prison."

"You're new here, so you don't see it yet," he said, leaning forward. He spread his hands wide, palms facing up, as if trying to encompass the entire room. "These walls—they keep us safe. They're not here to trap us." His hands then formed a barrier in front of him, fingers interlocking, before slowly pulling apart, illustrating the walls coming down. "One day, these walls will fall, and everything will go back to how it was. Just wait and see," he said, his fingers unfurling like petals opening to the sun, a gesture full of hope and promise.

Teddy stared at him. "Are you trying to convince me, or yourself?"

Perry fell silent. Teddy looked down at his bowl of soup, and his stomach growled. Just as he was about to give in to his stinging throat's demands, a shrill tone emitted from the overhead system.

"Well, that's the bell," Perry said as he grabbed his tray and stood up. "We have to go."

"Attention, the dining hall is now closed," the voice over the PA announced. "Bus your trays and report to your work detail or dormitory immediately."

"Fuck it." Teddy picked up the bowl of soup, slurped the noxious concoction down, and prayed it wouldn't come back up.

"Wise choice," Perry said.

Teddy pinched his nose shut and gulped the cup of water down in one go. His body attempted to reject it, but he swallowed the acidic taste and burped.

"Another wise choice."

"Time will tell." Teddy said as he woozily got to his feet and picked up his tray.

"Clear the dining hall and report to your work detail," the voice over the PA insisted. "Community regulations reminder: failure to comply with official instructions is a punishable offense."

"Let's go!" one officer shouted as the last few people headed toward the door. "Get moving!"

"I'll take you to your staging area," Perry said. "It's near the warehouse at the rear gate."

Teddy followed Perry and dumped his tray in one of the black wash basins by the exit. The chilly morning air forced his hands into his coat pockets. Despite the ebb and flow of conversation and the sound of children's laughter, there was a palpable tension in the air that, once again, was all too familiar.

They walked along a winding path through makeshift bazaars and gambling huts full of elderly people. Children ran out of the ramshackle shops and pushed their wares on passersby. Winter coats, gloves, and blankets appeared to be in high demand, and were offered in exchange for canned goods and jewelry. However, none of the children approached as soon as they saw Perry's red armband.

Teddy studied their frightened faces as the children retreated. "What do the kids do all day?"

"Until they get a school up and running, they just get into trouble," Perry said with a grin. "Kids, old folks, the feeble-minded, and some mothers don't have work assignments, so they stay here all day."

"A daycare center, retirement home, and prison all rolled into one ugly package," Teddy said.

"That's pessimistic, but I guess I can understand why you'd see it that way."

They turned a corner and arrived at a section closed in by chain-link fences, and that hosted a few turnstiles. Razor wire topped the fence, and officers wearing riot gear stood guard. A sign hung on the fence: *VEHICLE STAGING ZONE—AUTHORIZED INDIVIDUALS ONLY PAST THIS POINT—USE OF DEADLY FORCE AUTHORIZED.* People passed through the turnstiles one at a time after one of the attending officers scanned their wrists.

"This is where we say goodbye," Perry said as they came to a stop on the footpath.

The rear gate awaited just past the turnstiles, where rows of white busses adorned with the Department of Homeland Security logo idled;

all of their windows were blacked out. A handful of people lined up to board, and officers distributed rubber gloves, reflective safety vests, and flimsy dust masks.

"Community notice," the voice echoed over the PA. "Work call is commencing. Report to your detail supervisor. Failure to perform your assigned duties is a punishable offense."

Packed buses were escorted through the heavily fortified vehicular sally port, hosed off with disinfectant, and then given the all-clear to head down a dirt road that stretched off into the horizon. Teddy couldn't help but notice that most of the men and women waiting to board appeared to be in poor health—many had sores and coughed violently. He prayed Ein wasn't one of the unlucky bastards on one of those buses.

"You'll be reporting here every day, so I hope you remember how we got here."

"I'm sure I'll figure it out."

"Well, you best get to it. I'll see you this evening." Perry turned and started to walk away, but stopped and looked back over his shoulder. "While you're out there, look around. Maybe then you'll understand that it's not so bad in here."

"I don't think I'm the one who's looking at it all wrong, my friend." Teddy headed towards the turnstile, but an officer blocked his path by extending a hand.

"Hold up," the officer ordered. A gas mask muffled his husky voice. "I have to scan you."

"I'm from dorm twenty," Teddy said.

"Good for you," the officer replied sarcastically. "Everyone has to get scanned."

He snatched up Teddy's wrist, pulled his arm forward, and scanned his implant with a handheld device. He stared down at the screen and then let go; Teddy rubbed his wrist, frowning.

"Teddy Sanders: dorm twenty," the officer read from the screen. "Your bus today is number six hundred and nine." He turned and pointed at one of the last remaining vehicles idling with its doors open. "Looks like everyone is waiting for you. Your sarge is going to be pissed."

"First day here and I'm already making friends," Teddy grumbled.

As soon as he passed through the turnstile, a nozzle mounted on the fence above his head sprayed Teddy with disinfectant. His eyes stung as he coughed, and the droplets felt like icy barbs against his skin. As he approached the bus, he saw an officer waiting by its door and holding a pair of yellow gloves, an orange vest, and a dust mask. The officer was a young, clean-shaven Asian man with a bald head and a frostbitten face.

His helmet was askew, and the embroidered name on his jacket read *P. VUE.*

"Sorry I'm late," Teddy said as he neared. "I got a little turned around trying to find this place."

"Yo, excuses are like assholes—everyone has one," Officer Vue said with a slight Brooklyn-based inflection in his voice. He turned his head toward the open bus doors. "Sergeant Parham! The new dude finally showed up!"

A short, African American man with a push broom mustache and small eyes emerged and glowered at Teddy. His pressed uniform bore sergeant's insignias. His black boots, polished to a mirror finish, didn't appear to have ever seen a day of combat. He wore a patent leather duty belt and a black beret. Parham puffed his chest out, clenched his fists, and stormed off the bus to confront Teddy.

"Boss, I'm sorry for being late."

As soon as he was within range, Parham punched him hard in the center of his chest. Teddy dropped to his knees and gasped as all the air rushed from his lungs. He felt his face turning red as he struggled to breathe, and he clutched his chest, wheezing.

"That was from Lieutenant Hock," Parham said with a twang in his voice. "Special request."

With no more explanation, Parham drove a knee into his face. Blood shot out of Teddy's nose as his head snapped back, and he collapsed with his arms sprawled at his sides.

"That was from me," Parham sneered. "My time is valuable. Don't be fucking late next time!"

Teddy coughed up strings of mucus and slowly rolled over onto his hands and knees, blood dripping from his nose. Parham grabbed him by the collar and yanked him up to his feet. Disoriented and dizzy, Teddy felt surprised by the short man's strength. He stumbled forward as he wiped his nose. It took every inch of restraint not to turn around and strike back, but he knew that would only end badly for him. He had to keep pushing forward. He had to find Ein and escape.

Vue shoved a reflective vest, yellow rubber gloves, and a crumpled dust mask at Teddy's chest. "Real simple, yo. Be on time next time."

Teddy strolled up the steps with his gear and entered the bus, which immediately reminded him of a prisoner transport vehicle. The stale air reeked of body odor as warm air blasted out of the overhead vents. A security grille sectioned rows of seats off from the front of the bus. Two rows of seats where the officers sat were outside of the grille, and their windows weren't blacked-out like all the others. Teddy stared at the back of the bus and saw the sunken faces staring back at him—every seat looked occupied.

A burly white officer sat in the driver's seat wearing black tactical pants and a polo shirt. His greasy hair was slicked back, and he had a long, bushy beard. *FEDERAL POLICE* was printed across the back of his shirt, and *J. SALGUERO* was on his front left breast pocket.

"Kick rocks, dumbass. Find a seat," Salguero ordered as he jerked his thumb over his shoulder. "Don't worry. Those pussies back there don't bite."

Teddy walked down the narrow aisle, clutching his gear. He felt like the new kid in school; all eyes were on him and his bloodied nose.

It's going to be a long day.

He stopped in the middle of the aisle and searched for an open seat. Behind him, Parham and Vue boarded the bus. They slammed the grille shut, locked it, and took seats across from one another.

"New marching orders," Parham told Salguero as he fastened his seatbelt. He plucked a red folder from the seat next to him that read, *DAILY OPERATIONAL SCHEDULE.* He flipped it open and scanned over the paper inside. "Take us to 10th and Jackson in downtown: the old government district."

"No more residential?" Vue asked the sergeant.

"Plenty more, just none today," Parham said as he put the folder away.

"Thank God," Vue said with obvious relief. He placed his rifle across his lap. "Man, those apartments smelled like straight shit! Even gas masks don't help."

"Burn the whole rotting city down and start over, I say," Salguero muttered as he gazed vacantly ahead.

"Just get us out of here." Parham leaned his head back and closed his eyes. "We're already late."

Salguero picked up a radio and pulled the lever to fold the bus doors shut. "Transport six-zero-nine to Jayhawk Control: permission to disembark? All souls present and accounted for."

"Jayhawk Control copies: six-zero-nine. All clear—proceed to the gate," a tired voice responded.

The bus jerked forward as the vehicle started moving. Teddy stumbled, but caught himself on the seatback. A man wearing an oversize jacket covered with burlap patches motioned Teddy over. A wool cap covered his long, red hair, and a stringy goatee clung to his pale chin. His nose was bulbous and red.

"Window seat open over here, hoss," the man said in a thick Midwestern accent.

Teddy walked over, slid past him, and plopped down on the seat. "Thanks."

"You betcha! Window seats get chilly. I prefer the aisle."

The window was painted black from the inside, so only a few rogue beams of sunlight filtered through areas where the paint had been scratched away.

"Not much of a view," Teddy said.

"None at all," the man replied with a grin. "I promised you a window, but I never said anything about a view, now did I?" He extended his hand. "Name's Roger."

"Teddy," he answered as he shook the man's hand.

"Nice to meetcha, Teddy. I—"

Vue kicked the security grille. "No socializing back there! No talking!"

They fell silent, but Roger rolled his eyes and made a jerking motion with his left hand. Teddy grinned and turned to his blackened window. As the bus moved through the sally port, he heard the disinfectant wash over the exterior and pelt the glass. He reached up and stealthily scratched some of the black paint off of the glass with his fingernail. He peered through the tiny hole he made and saw a group of officers armed to the teeth wearing protective gear standing guard as people in white biohazard suits hosed the bus down. A gun turret was positioned just outside the fence, its high-caliber barrels trained on the bus, and a watchtower with an array of spotlights stood nearby.

The security detail appeared formidable; Teddy would never make it through the rear gate. He would have to think of another way to escape.

The bus cleared the sally port and sped down the country road. The full expanse of the camp came into view. Concrete watchtowers had been erected every two hundred yards or so, and the chain-link fence stretched out for miles. Behind the fence, countless dormitories were indistinguishable from one another. The camp disappeared from view as the road cut through a solar farm.

He leaned his head back against the headrest and sighed as he surveyed the sprawling compound. Finding Ein would be a herculean task, maybe even impossible, but he was determined not to give up.

I'll find you, kid.

5

Almost two hours had passed since they left the camp. Teddy stared out of his makeshift peephole at the depressing remnants of life.

Rusty cars and piles of moldering trash had been pushed to both sides of the Kansas Turnpike. Aside from an initial plowing to create a pathway for FEMA convoys, it didn't appear that cleaning and decontaminating the interstate was high on anyone's list of priorities, so nature had taken its course. Skeletal corpses sat frozen behind steering wheels and slumped across rotting dashboards. However, the abasement did not confine itself to the highway; overgrown, frosty fields stretched out for miles, and perennial, woody vines encroached on the abandoned farmhouses and boarded-up homesteads peppering the barren land. Tractors sunk into the earth on rotting tires, and forgotten stables housed the remains of horses and livestock that had long since succumbed to starvation.

Between the silence inside the bus and the decaying world outside, Teddy found a strange sort of peace. The haunting stillness that surrounded him was a welcome change from the whirlwind of chaos that had followed him since Tucson. Transfixed by the scenery, he found a brief respite from Jane's memory, as well as all the others he had left behind.

As they drove on, the overgrown fields and farmhouses gave way to empty neighborhoods and shuttered strip malls. Torn billboards lined the freeway, while wrecked vehicles, overgrown plants, and fallen trees rendered the side streets impassable. Loose paper and mounds of trash flooded the alleyways and sidewalks. Teddy could tell that they were getting close to a major city, but he had no clue which one.

At the front of the bus, Parham and Vue stood up, donned their gas masks, and checked the filters. Teddy looked away from the window and cradled his head in his hands, sighing.

"You look nervous, but you don't need to be," Roger whispered. "I was shaky the first time I went out, too."

Those seated nearby remained silent as they scowled and kept their heads down.

Teddy lowered his hands. "I'm not nervous. I'm just irritated that I'm sitting here freezing my ass off under the watch of that short piece of shit standing up front."

Roger offered him a thin smile. "You'll get used to it—both the cold and Parham's delightful personality." He pointed at Teddy's bruised and bloodied nose. "Parham's work? He's got a real bad case of the holler tail. Nasty one, that's for sure."

"Yeah, I noticed." He reached up and rubbed the dry flakes of blood off of his upper lip. "I seem to have that effect on people."

"I know the feeling, buddy." Roger chuckled. "I ran a pawn shop before the bug hit—not the best profession to make friends in. What did you do?"

"Security," Teddy said. "Banks, mostly."

Vue pounded the grille with his fist. "Yo! Shut up back there!"

Roger lowered his head and placed his index finger against his pursed lips with wide comical eyes and shushed him. Teddy grinned.

"Listen up!" Parham announced, voice muffled by his mask. "The priority today will be the Kansas State Capitol. City leaders require a centralized location. Since the building was closed for the duration of the pandemic, we don't expect many corpses. It *is* located outside the safe zone, so there is no telling who crept in and has since died. If you find a corpse, deal with it. There will be a flatbed coming and a security team from the city will work alongside you today, sweeping the area for any survivors. As always, if you encounter a survivor, let the security team deal with them—do not engage. Your mission is to perform power restoration preparation protocols before the block gets placed back on the grid and then absorbed into the safe zone. Full power restoration is scheduled in two days."

"Power restoration protocols?" Teddy whispered to Roger.

"Easy day," Roger whispered back.

Parham scowled at Teddy. "Since we have a recruit, I will remind you all that the control center in the safe zone will monitor your chips, and they will track your movements. If you try to run, you will be tracked down and executed. Does anybody have questions?" Parham ignored Teddy's icy glare and adjusted his gas mask's straps. "Good. Gear up and get ready—we're almost there."

The other passengers put on their reflective vests, gloves, and ill-fitting dust masks as they anxiously shifted in their seats.

"You'll be paired off," Vue said. "The person you're sitting with is who you'll be working with!"

Teddy put on his vest and gloves before looking over at Roger. "I hope you know what the hell you're doing, because I was never much of an electrician."

"It doesn't take a doctorate degree to unplug a coffee maker," Roger said with a grin. "But if you get confused, I'll help you out."

"Thanks, you're a real lifesaver."

Roger laughed. "Just relax. Power restores are easy. All we have to do is walk around and unplug whatever folks left on before they died. A coffee maker or space heater left unattended could start a fire, and that's never good."

"What if we come across a dead body?" Teddy asked.

"We pretend we didn't." Roger shot him a goofy grin and put his mask on.

Teddy chuckled and looked back out the window. The bus pulled off the freeway and onto a street that probably used to be the downtown area. A wall constructed from interlocking steel slats separated many of the buildings from the rest of the city, running along side streets and alleyways and zigzagging between abandoned structures. Razor wire topped the wall, with spotlights and makeshift watchtowers mounted on slab scissor lifts monitoring the area. Flatbeds loaded with additional steel slats parked near the watchtowers stood ready to modify the modular wall at a moment's notice. The steel barrier bore the stenciled message, TOPEKA SAFE ZONE.

Inside the walled complex, repaired windows lined the buildings and the streetlights worked. Steam rose from the HVAC systems, and FEMA officers patrolled the rooftops, monitoring the people below. Electric lights gleamed from mid-rise apartment buildings and office towers, many bordered by scaffolding as workers repainted them and repaired damage from the riots caused by the outbreak.

Outside the wall, things looked much different—the dark streets were littered with rusted, abandoned vehicles. The windows of derelict buildings had been shattered, and yellowed sheets hung from balconies with handwritten messages pleading for help.

Teddy surveyed it all with raised eyebrows. "That is…something."

"I guess you can see why folks want to live there. Too bad the rest of the city isn't so picturesque yet."

"Who rebuilt everything?"

"We did—the vultures. Teams just like ours made all that possible. Every week, that steel wall extends and envelops more buildings."

"I didn't expect much progress," Teddy said. "The last time I was in a city, it looked like a war zone."

"Most still do. For every city they reclaim, just think about how many small towns get left behind."

Teddy peered at one of the office buildings that was getting its windows power washed. "Do the people who still live here work a nine-to-five at some office, go home, and pretend that everything is normal?"

"Nah, I don't think they're that sheltered," Roger said. "I heard that they have to work just like we do. They run the factories, power plants, and do most of the manufacturing work. Outside of skilled labor, most of the medical folks and cops live in the city."

"So it's a just another work camp…"

"Yeah, but with nicer beds and better food, I suppose."

Teddy frowned. "I'd pass on it if they offered."

"Judging by how you make friends, I don't see you getting an invitation soon, hoss. If they offered it, I wouldn't brush it off," Roger mused. "I've heard it's a different quality of life inside."

Teddy turned his attention back to what was happening on the other side of the window and glanced up at one of snipers standing on a watchtower platform. "I'm not fond of being kept inside by walls and men with guns."

"It's just the way things are now," Roger said.

"A cage is still a cage." Teddy looked over at Roger. "What happens to the others?"

"Others?"

"The ones who refuse to live in a work camp or a safe zone."

Roger thought for a moment and then shrugged. "I'm not sure there are too many decent folks left. Beyond the city, life is dangerous. Terrorists have claimed all the remaining land."

"Terrorists?"

"Separatists, nutjobs…whatever you want to call them," Roger said as he scratched his red nose. "They figured they were just fine without a government and want it to stay that way. Dying over an ideology makes about as much sense to me as government cheese; nobody cares and they're only hurting the folks living in the city with their attacks."

"I've slept with one eye open long enough. That type of lifestyle just doesn't suit me anymore."

"If the bed was nice enough, I'd happily lay down with one eye open all night long."

"Now you sound like Perry."

"Old Perry? The orderly?" Roger shook his head. "That doormat licks the cops' boot heels every day when he puts on that stupid armband. Please don't insult me like that. I'm not saying that they are our saviors, but a free bowl of sour soup beats getting into a fistfight over a can of beans."

Teddy stared at the wall and watchtowers, and his frown deepened—it reminded him too much of USP Tucson. "I understand, but I couldn't live in a place like this. I want to scratch my nuts without Big Brother watching me."

Roger laughed, and his rosy cheeks filled with wrinkles. "If they wanted to get their jollies watching my old ass, I wouldn't stop them."

"You'd sell your dignity for a clean bed, huh?"

"Dignity? I already told you I ran a pawn shop. I gave up on dignity a long time ago."

Both men laughed, but it was short-lived.

"Quiet!" Vue ordered.

The bus turned a corner and came to an abrupt stop. The doors folded open and Parham stepped outside. Vue unlocked the security grille with a large, brass Folger Adam key and motioned for the passengers to step forward. He held a box of cheap plastic flashlights under his arm.

"Hurry up!" Vue said, his accent muffled by the gas mask. "One flashlight per group, and I better get it back at the end of the day!"

The passengers shuffled down the narrow aisle, and many of them coughed behind their flimsy masks. Vue handed a flashlight to every other person who passed.

Teddy followed Roger and adjusted his mask, realizing that the others kept their heads down and didn't speak. "Not a lively bunch, are they?"

Roger shushed him quietly as he walked with his eyes on the ground. Vue handed him a flashlight, but as soon as Teddy neared, Vue reached out and jabbed him in the chest. Teddy grunted and froze.

"Yo, if you talk so much on the way home, I'll make sure you won't be able to move your jaw," Vue warned. "No side conversations—that's the rule. Got it?"

"Yeah," Teddy croaked. "I get it."

Satisfied, Vue stepped aside and allowed Teddy to pass.

Through the windshield, Teddy saw that the bus was parked in front of a large courtyard. The Kansas State Capitol stood on the other side.

Salguero gave Teddy a sideways glance from the driver's seat. "You won't last a week."

Teddy looked down at the unarmed driver; the man was a joke. Despite dressing as if he were going to battle, he didn't even possess a pistol.

"Just be a good chauffeur and keep it nice and warm in here."

He walked down the steps when Salguero thrust his foot against Teddy's back, sending him flying forward to land hard on the asphalt. Teddy coughed violently, wrapping his arms around his bruised ribs.

"Careful on that last step," Salguero said with a dark grin.

Roger bent to help him up. "For crying out loud. Stop ruffling their feathers."

"Is there a problem?" Parham asked as he walked over, his rifle at the ready.

Teddy rose to his feet, shook his head, then pulled his mask down to spit out a wad of bloody mucus.

"Then get your ass moving!" Parham ordered.

He snatched Teddy by the back of his neck and pushed him away from the bus and toward the courtyard. Roger hurried after him. Teddy clenched his fists and spun toward Parham, who stepped back and pointed his rifle at Teddy.

Roger stepped between them and forced a smile. "Don't worry, boss, I'll keep an eye on him and make a decent laborer out of him yet!" He jerked a thumb over his shoulder at Teddy. "He's still all schnookered from last night, that's all!"

Before Parham could answer, Roger led Teddy off the road and into the courtyard proper, where frozen, dying grass was boxed in by overgrown hedges. Brown vines crept up the park benches and covered the broken marble fountain in the center. Barren trees rustled in the bitter wind, and a few still lay where they'd toppled across the footpaths.

Beyond the courtyard, sunlight glimmered off of the Capitol's iconic dome, but the rest of the building appeared to be in a state of severe disrepair. Graffiti covered most of the limestone along the lower levels. The glass in all but one window had been shattered. Two marble support pillars had broken and lay in pieces on the stone steps leading up to the entrance.

"Thanks for that back there," Teddy said once they were out of Parham's earshot. "I'm not very good at keeping my cool."

"I can tell." Roger chuckled. He turned on his flashlight briefly. Satisfied that it was in working order, he turned it off again and stuck it in his back pocket. "Learn to bite your tongue. Those fools think they're the Frozen Chosen and are itching for an excuse to pull their triggers."

"I've tried to be civil, but they all have massive power trips—

especially that motherfucking sergeant."

"Parham? Yeah, most short men do."

"And what's with that bullshit no talking rule that the Asian guy was going on about?"

"It's exactly what you said it is. Bullshit," Roger said. "They're just making up rules for the hell of it."

"Jesus…I would have been better off just staying where I was."

He looked over at a row of newspaper vending racks owned by *The Kansas City Star*. A yellowed piece of paper dated from months ago stood in one of the glass displays and had an image of corpses stacked outside a hospital. *Harlem Flu Overwhelms Topeka Hospitals—Local Government Mum on Official Death Toll.*

"Where were you before?" Roger asked.

"Before what?"

"Before the camp."

"A stadium," Teddy said.

"You stayed in a stadium? Hot dogs, popcorn: you were lucky! Ours was at a high school in Topeka."

"It wasn't anything special." Teddy shrugged. "It was just a dirty cesspool."

"Really?"

"Yeah, what else would you expect?" Teddy asked. "They brought people there by force."

"Yeah, that's a good point," Roger admitted. "If I had my druthers, I'd still be back at my ranch. Honestly, the high school wasn't so bad. It was cleaner than the camp, and most of the folks were downright friendly. I sure miss some of them. I hope they're doing well wherever they ended up."

As Teddy thought about his time in the stadium, his mind drifted to Jane and Danny. Their memories plagued his consciousness even when he was awake.

Roger glanced over at him. "What's wrong?" When Teddy didn't respond, Roger grew flustered and scratched his neck, embarrassed. "Ah. Sorry. Didn't mean to pick at scabs. I shouldn't have brought it up. I've lost people, too, both before and after the high school."

Teddy thought about Ein. "Here lately, all I seem to do is lose people." He heaved a sigh. "You'd think I'd be used to it by now."

"It never gets easy, and you'll never get used to it. All you can do is keep moving forward."

"I didn't take you as the inspirational speeches type, Roger."

Roger laughed. "Get some liquor in me, and I'll preach the gospel to you.”

Teddy grinned. Despite the grim surroundings and his even grimmer mood, he found a strange sense of comfort in Roger’s goofy company. Roger, seemingly unaware that Teddy was looking at him, picked his bulbous nose and crossed the street to get to the Capitol’s steps.

A black Humvee parked in the clearing nearby had an array of loudspeakers fastened to a pole on its roof. The Department of Homeland Security’s emblem adorned the doors, and the words “Topeka Federal Police” were stenciled across its fenders. Blue lights flashed brightly from the bar across its roof. A voice boomed over its loudspeakers.

“Attention, any squatters in the area: this is the Topeka Federal Police. Surrender immediately for medical evaluation, or you will be subject to detention. Repeat: surrender immediately or you will be detained by force.”

Two black prisoner vans pulled up with their emergency lights flashing and came to a stop on opposite sides of the street. Police wearing helmets and gas masks hopped out of the back of the vehicles and ran up the steps into the Capitol with their shotguns ready.

“It looks like they’re ready for war,” Teddy said.

“Always goes this way,” Roger replied with a shrug. “It doesn’t matter how peacefully they surrender—force is always used.”

“And what if they are sick?”

“Do you really have to ask?”

“None of this is right,” Teddy murmured, almost as if he were talking to himself instead of Roger.

“No, it’s not, but let’s keep moving.”

A swarm of low-flying drones emerged from the safe zone and converged on the courtyard and the surrounding area. They flew low and fast as they scanned the rooftops and peered down alleyways. Teddy ducked and then looked up, confused. He had been locked up for a very long time, so this was the first time he had seen a drone in action.

“Come on,” Roger said with a smile. “They won’t hurt you. All they do is look for squatters and make sure none of us run off.” He pointed up at one. “See the lens there at the bottom?”

“Little flying cameras?” Teddy asked as he rose back up. He shook his head and started walking again. “Shit, I guess I really was better off at that awful stadium.”

Teddy and Roger followed the other workers from the bus up the stairs and through the building’s massive wooden doors. In front of the old metal detectors, a sign read, *Public Building Closed by Order of the Kansas*

Department of Health.

Loose trash littered the marble floor of the building's grand hall and rotunda. Rogue sunlight streamed through the dome's skylights, casting long shadows across makeshift encampments built from office furniture and tattered sheets. Graffiti covered most of the art déco murals on the walls, which peeled away from the stucco due to exposure to the elements. In the center of the rotunda, a gigantic marble Lady Justice stood with the Kansas flag draped over her scales—her other hand's sword had been smashed to pieces, presumably by vandals.

"Well, so much for the place being untouched since it closed," Teddy said as he surveyed the tents.

The sound of people shouting and scuffling with officers echoed through the rotunda.

"Yep," Roger said as he walked forward and stood next to Teddy. "It also sounds like the place hasn't been abandoned after all."

One of the nearby restroom doors flung open, and a riot officer dragged a screaming woman by her long, red hair. He yanked her across the floor with one hand as she held onto his wrist and flailed her legs, kicking off one of her scuffed tennis shoes in the process. Another officer escorted a frail-looking man out with his arms twisted behind his back.

"Come on." Roger pointed toward a group of office doors under a brass placard that read, *Public Records Division.* "Let's get away from the circus before we get stuck with the clowns."

"Good idea."

Teddy tried multiple doors until he found one that was unlocked. It was pitch-black inside. Roger followed him and pulled out his flashlight. He turned it on and scanned the room with its dim, yellow light.

Cubicles lined one side of the room, while tall filing cabinets lined the other. Most of the cabinet drawers were open, and loose papers and folders lay scattered across the floor. Office chairs and fallen ceiling tiles created a mild obstacle course along the narrow pathway down the center of the room. The dusty desks still had computers, and many of the workstations even had purses, backpacks, and the moldering remains of unfinished breakfasts and snacks still sitting on them.

"It looks like everyone was in a hurry to leave."

"When people started realizing how bad it really was, a single cough could clear an entire room," Roger said. "The panic and paranoia was almost as bad as the flu itself. Folks were either jumping at their own shadows or hustling on the street, selling snake oils just to make a few damn dollars from the sick and dying."

"I guess I was spared from the worst of it, all things considered."

"How do you figure?"

"Never was much for watching the news, and I didn't buy into rumors. I kept my head down, but that came at a price. I didn't even know what was happening until it was literally all around me."

"So you lived rural, huh?"

"You could say that. I liked my solitude…my routine. I miss how simple life was."

"No offense, but I didn't take you for a country boy," Roger said with a grin. "Where are you from?"

"Texas, originally," Teddy said as he started walking again. "I was living outside Tucson when the bug hit. You?"

"I'm country, through and through," Roger said proudly. "Lived on my family's ranch outside Topeka since I was knee-high in hog shit."

"A ranch in the middle of Kansas?" Teddy whistled. "I guess the post-apocalypse lifestyle is an improvement for you, then?"

"Watch it, hoss," Roger said with a chuckle. "I know more than a thousand insults about Texans, but I don't want to hurt your feelings on your first day."

Both men laughed and walked deeper into the room.

Roger's flashlight revealed family photographs and mementos tacked to the cubical walls—photographs of people who were most likely decaying in a mass grave somewhere. Teddy plucked a photograph of a smiling family of four from one of the walls and studied it with a frown. The boy looked to be about Danny's age.

"It's hard to believe just how fast things changed."

"It is," Roger patted Teddy on the back, "but it's no use reminiscing. Let's keep moving along."

Teddy pinned the picture back up and looked at the computer on the desk. "Shouldn't we be unplugging all the computers and whatnot?"

"We should, but we ain't," Roger answered as he kept walking.

"I don't get it." He gave his back a quizzical glance, but followed him.

"What's not to get? They want us to do a lot of work, and I'm not fond of working for free." He scanned the room with his light. "Plus, they don't even give us lunch, and that really doesn't sit well with me."

"So what do you do for the whole shift?"

"If I get paired off with the right person, I find a quiet room that's out of the way so no nosy cops or do-gooders disturb me. After that, I kick back until they blow the signal for us to head back." He started walking toward a row of closed office doors past the file cabinets. "Like I told you, it's an easy day since we're working inside."

"I'm not a fan of laziness, but I'm not a fan of working for free either," Teddy said with a smirk.

Roger chuckled. "I figured we'd be in agreement on that." He pointed at his implant. "We'll have to get up and move around now and then so that it doesn't look too suspicious, but I doubt that the people watching the screens are really paying much attention. They're more concerned about people leaving the work zone. Escapes and all that, you know?"

Teddy looked down at the bulge under his forearm where the implant was located and sighed. "Man, I feel so left behind with all this technology bullshit."

"It isn't hard to figure out," Roger said. "If my old, country ass can figure it out, you can, too." He led Teddy around a corner toward a larger area that had private offices and a break room, then focused his flashlight on the nearest closed door. "Think this one is a winner?"

"Let's see." Teddy sauntered over, turned the knob, and swung the door open.

A musky scent of decay wafted to them from the dark office. The decrepit remains of a man wearing a gray suit was propped up in his chair behind a massive desk. He peered out at them with hollowed eyes and a skeletal grin. Wads of used tissues covered the desk and were scattered on the floor.

"Poor bastard." Teddy cupped a hand over his mask, tightening the seal. "Should we move him?"

"We should, but we ain't." Roger pointed the light at another closed door. "Let's try door number two."

Teddy shut the door, walked over to the next room, and turned the knob. Roger pointed his flashlight inside.

Tall, beige filing cabinets lined the rear wall, and blueprints were stacked on top of a wooden desk in the middle of the room. A door in the corner bore a tarnished brass sign that read, *35mm slide storage*. It seemed like nobody had used the room for a very long time.

"Winner, winner, chicken dinner!" Roger exclaimed happily as he stepped inside. Teddy followed somewhat reluctantly, hesitating and glancing over his shoulder. But Roger would have none of that. "Don't be a hayseed and just stand there! Close the door before someone else finds this."

Teddy did as he asked and then looked at Roger with a frown. "Are you sure they won't find us in here? I'm mighty tired of getting my ass kicked around by power-hungry goons."

"The only two things in life I'm sure of is that I'm not getting any prettier and I'm not getting richer. Anything else, I couldn't tell you one way or the other," Roger said with a shrug. "All I know is that I haven't gotten caught yet, so the odds must be in my favor!"

Roger shoved the blueprints off the desk, sending them tumbling to the floor. A giant plume of dust rose from the sudden movement. Teddy waved his hand in front of his face, coughing behind his ineffective mask.

Roger left the flashlight on and placed it on the table. It lit up the room with a dim, yellow glow. An uneasy quiet filled the room, but in the distance, muffled shouts and cries for help could be heard as officers apprehended squatters.

Teddy found the tense atmosphere unsettling, yet also familiar. "So what do we do now?"

Roger pulled out a weathered deck of playing cards and started shuffling. "Do you know how to play gin rummy?"

"No."

"You're gonna," Roger said with a grin.

6

Mark Hammond sat at a round table in what was once someone's dining room. The dusty drapes were pulled shut across the windows, blocking out the afternoon sun. An ornate grandfather clock stood in the corner, its brass pendulum dutifully marking the passing seconds.

Of all the other rooms in the drab, depressing house, Hammond hated the dining room most of all. It was where the higher-ups summoned him when they had bad news. When the red phone rang in his office that day—November twenty-fifth, just after one o'clock in the afternoon—it was just as he expected. Bad news had arrived.

Hammond slouched at the only seat at the table, which was surrounded by monitors suspended from the ceiling. Two agents from his personal security detail stood solemnly behind him with their hands behind their backs. After the men on the screens finished speaking for what felt like hours, an uncomfortable silence lingered in the air. The repetitive ticking of the grandfather clock only served to make things worse.

They waited for his response, but Hammond stared impassively at the monitors. The generals all wore dress uniforms decked out with full regalia. Hammond, meanwhile, wore nothing more than his bathrobe and some slippers. He felt underdressed, but he really didn't care.

What bothered him were the looks of disgusted pity he was getting. They stared at him as if he were the drunken uncle that had ruined yet another family reunion, or as if he were some senile geriatric they were tasked with caring for while he did nothing more than waste away and defecate himself. Didn't they know he was once just like them? He hadn't always been a lush drowning his depression in whiskey. At one point, he possessed money. At one point, he held power. He once—

"Do you understand the implications, Director Hammond?" one general asked, breaking him out of his train of thought.

Hammond frowned at the half-witted question. After all, it wasn't that hard to figure out.

There was an outbreak of cholera and typhoid at another camp—what else was new? What made matters worse was the fact that those anti-government separatist assholes were riling people up. Judging by the drone footage Hammond had seen, there was a fine shit show unfolding over at Director Moll's camp in Nebraska. Things were falling apart, and if the camp fell, then the city they were reconstructing would be the next domino in line. Apparently, nobody at the top wanted to risk losing the fine city of Lincoln, Nebraska.

God only knew why. In Hammond's mind, Lincoln was about as worthless as Topeka, and both were insignificant dots on flyover states.

Moll's camp needed more troops, ammunition, and food: three things that Hammond's camp needed itself.

A real fine shit show indeed.

Resources were to be diverted from Hammond's camp since his was the closest and, according to the talking heads on the screens, had fewer security issues. It was an ill-conceived decision made by a bureaucratic hive mind tucked underground in a government bunker hundreds of miles away.

Nobody asked Hammond what he thought—they never did. They had forgotten about him as soon as they stuck him in an old farmhouse smack-dab in the middle of nowhere.

"Director Hammond!" the general shouted. "Do you understand the implications?"

Hammond looked at the screen. The old general stared back with a reddened face and beady, green eyes. Liver spots covered his bald head, and wrinkles lined his cheeks. It was ironic that the virus had spared the cantankerous old man, but saw fit to destroy his beautiful Laura.

For a brief second, he saw her ghostly visage in his mind's eye. He saw her pallid face. He felt the pillow in his hands.

Hammond swallowed hard and pushed the images out of his mind. He'd never needed a drink as badly as he did at that moment.

"I do..." He ran his fingers through his disheveled hair and attempted to slick it back off of his face. "It's going to be a hard sell on my end..."

"Your people are compliant enough," liver spots sneered.

"That's because they're fed," Hammond spiritlessly replied. "If you take away the only leverage I have, I am not sure that will hold true much longer."

"This isn't a negotiation," one of the other generals replied in a cold and direct tone. "You have a surplus of food, which is more than any other camp in the region can say. Logistically speaking, diverting from your camp makes the most sense. This is a temporary problem that will be resolved quickly."

Hammond stared at the stern man with the crew cut and knew that he was lying. Problems of this magnitude were rarely temporary, and seldom resolved.

At the onset of the pandemic, silly platitudes had concealed from the public the dangers of the virus. Hammond recalled assuring his own constituents in packed town halls that things would be resolved quickly, and that those who were sick would recover if they followed the CDC's advice. He knew all the tired lines, and it aggravated him that the man on the screen was trying to use one on him. Did they assume he was a simpleton who would be pacified by this utter nonsense?

"The people don't understand logistics," he said in a cross voice that surprised even him with its vehemence. "They understand food."

"They'll still have food," a young general chimed in, "just not as much. Implement winter rations: one high-caloric meal a day. Once things settle and we refurbish the supplies, things can return to normal."

Hammond regarded the fresh-faced general and the sly smirk on the kid's lips. How many veterans had to die from this sickness just so he could sit in a position he neither understood nor deserved?

"What about our Topeka settlement?" he asked.

"Topeka operations will continue," the older general responded. "Your fuel allotment for your motor fleet will continue as is."

"And what of the research division?"

"Continue the work at all costs," liver spots answered. "If research needs more people, let us know and we will send more trains."

"Will I get more troops to help manage any new civilians we take on?"

"If research needs more people, let us know and we will send more trains."

If the work was so important, then why upset the status quo? He needed more soldiers and food, not more fucking civilians to feed. He thought about pointing that out, but didn't think it would do any good.

"Speaking of the research," the stony-faced general with the crew cut interrupted. "Has there been any progress on that front?"

Hammond tried to recall what that researcher with the annoying voice had tried to impress him with, but he couldn't remember anything meaningful. He had been too drunk and too busy wallowing to pay attention to a bunch of scientific jargon.

"None that I know of."

The room fell silent for several moments as the grandfather clock ticked on unabated.

"In any case," general crew cut said, clearing his throat. "You have your new orders. Advise your security operations Lieutenant…" He looked down at a piece of paper, reading a name. "Lieutenant Hock."

As if he didn't know who his own fucking security operations lieutenant was. "When will they come to pick up the food surplus?"

"They're doing it right now," liver spots quickly replied.

Hammond looked at the screen, his mouth agape in the face of their audacity. No notice? No anything?

"Gentlemen," general crew cut said before Hammond could speak up. "This meeting is adjourned."

One by one the monitors went black, leaving Hammond sitting alone in a dark room. He sighed and pinched the bridge of his nose. Another migraine was coming—fast. Groaning like a man twice his age, he forced himself to get up and step out into the hallway. His security detail followed.

Shoulders drooping, he slowly made his way to the window. He placed an open palm against the chilly glass and peered out at the camp. As if on cue, two Boeing CH-47 Chinook transport helicopters ascended from helipads behind the central storage building.

"Bastards," Hammond whispered.

Both helicopters banked away from the camp and headed west. Seconds later, one of the camp's vehicle gates opened, and a Humvee sped along the dirt road and headed toward the farmhouse, leaving a plume of dust and bits of gravel in its wake. Hammond couldn't make out the face of the driver, but he was sure it was Hock coming to express his displeasure. He didn't feel like dealing with Hock, or anyone else, for that matter. He just wanted a drink and to be left alone.

He turned away from the window, yawned, and started shuffling back toward his chambers. He tightened the knot around his robe as he walked with all the grace and poise of a corpse. Hammond stopped and turned toward one of the men assigned to his security team.

"Go get me a drink," he ordered with a surprising amount of robustness in his voice.

The agent stared at him with an indignant expression and opened his mouth to object, but something about the look on Hammond's face made him turn and abruptly retreat.

Hammond's frustration with the generals, his anger regarding the food situation, and his annoyance with Hock's impending arrival faded into a mental haze. Slowly and insidiously, thoughts about Laura swam up from the murky depths of his subconscious.

God, I need a drink.

He winced and turned toward the man, who was already much further down the hallway.

"As a matter of fact," Hammond called out, "forget the glass and just bring the bottle!"

7

Hours passed, and yet, remarkably, the cheap plastic flashlight that sat in the middle of the table still emitted a soft, flickering glow. The light was dull and fading fast, but it lasted long enough to allow Teddy and Roger to play their gin rummy marathon uninterrupted. Teddy wasn't much of a card player, but he quickly caught on. He grinned when Roger was taken aback after he beat him during the second hour.

It was well past noon, and they had long since stopped keeping score; both men cracked jokes and chatted about the most trivial things, as if they were unwinding at some rundown bar after work with a drink in one hand and a cigar in the other.

It was a welcome change for Teddy. He was able to take his mind off of Ein, the virus, the camp, and even Jane—if only for a little while.

Then, like a shrill alarm clock intruding on a pleasant dream, a burst of gunfire from what sounded like a few rooms over from theirs and distant shouting brought Teddy crashing back to reality. There were no drinks or cigars—just a dusty old building full of molding corpses.

Roger folded his hand on the table. "Sounds like they're getting close. I figure we better cut this short and go pretend to do some work somewhere else."

"Reckon you're right," Teddy tossed his cards on the table and shrugged. "I didn't have anything good anyway."

"It wouldn't have mattered if you did," Roger said with a grin as he scooped up the cards and started putting them back into the case. "You wouldn't know how to play them!"

Teddy leaned back in his chair and crossed his arms over his chest with a smug smile. "I beat your crusty ass a few times, didn't I?"

"You got lucky," Roger quipped as he tucked the deck back into his pocket. "In fact—"

He was interrupted when the storage room door flung open and its doorknob crashed against the wall. Both Teddy and Roger jumped off of their seats and spun toward the door in shock. A middle-aged woman and a young girl bolted into the room, both breathing wildly.

The woman wore a tattered, dirty dress and a man's leather jacket. Her unkempt blonde hair was wild, and her bloodshot eyes were full of fear. Her deathly pale face was moist with sweat. The girl looked no older than eight and appeared just as dazed and disoriented as the woman did. A combination of sweat and tears ran down her chubby cheeks. Teddy's heart sank at the sight of the two wide-eyed strangers, and a hard knot formed in his throat; he couldn't help but see two familiar faces in theirs.

The woman slammed the door behind her and pressed her back against it, holding it shut.

Roger leaned closer to get a better look at them. "Lady, what are you—?"

"Please," the woman said in a raspy voice, "help us. The soldiers are chasing us."

A coughing spasm cut off anything she might have been about to add, and Roger yanked his mask on.

"Jesus, Teddy! She's sick."

"Please," the woman begged weakly. The girl clutched the woman's hand, her brow furrowed with worry, her eyes searching the woman's face for reassurance.

Roger studied the little girl's feverish face and took a step back. "The girl is sick, too…they both are."

Teddy had been on death's door himself not too long ago back in Tucson, and yet there he was—alive, ducking work, and playing gin rummy with some old rancher who had a penchant for trying to palm cards under the table. The fact that the woman and child were sick didn't mean much to him. The chances were slim, but they could still recover.

"They're both *sick*," Roger pointedly repeated.

Teddy turned and glared at him. "I can see that," he said with more venom than he'd intended. "What do we do?"

Roger studied the woman and child, thinking. They stared back at him with fearful expressions, waiting.

Teddy's anxiety ramped up as he heard the chatter of police radios getting closer. "Well?"

"If the cops get them, they're goners," Roger said with a frown.

"Where would they take them? Where's the nearest quarantine center?" Teddy asked.

Roger gave him a sorrowful look and shook his head. "There aren't any centers anymore. They don't deal with folks showing symptoms. They…take other measures."

"Then we have to do something," Teddy announced, nervously glancing around the room.

"Do what?"

"Anything!" Teddy bellowed. His eyes landed on the door marked with the placard. "Follow me—quietly."

The woman nodded and hurried behind him with the little girl in tow.

Roger picked up the flashlight and focused the dying beam on the storage room, but the beads of sweat forming on his brow were still visible in the relative darkness. "I don't like this, hoss."

"Yeah, well, I don't enjoy seeing innocent people get mowed down," Teddy said as he opened the door. "They deserve a chance. Shit, we had one, right?"

Roger didn't argue as Teddy ushered the woman and the girl into the dusty storage room and had them crouch down between stacks of old cardboard boxes that appeared to have been left untouched long before the virus struck.

"Stay here and keep quiet until I come get you. You're going to be safe. I promise."

The woman nodded, tears gleaming in her eyes. "Thank you."

Teddy shut the door, put on his mask, and went back out to Roger.

"Now what?" Roger asked.

"We wait."

The main door swung inward, and two officers wearing riot gear and gas masks peered into the room. Their stenciled breastplates read *"Topeka Federal Police"* along with their unit number. The officers pointed their tactical lights into the room. Two dazzling rays pierced the semidarkness of the room. Teddy and Roger squinted and shielded their faces with their palms. The yellow strips on their reflective safety vests shimmered under the bright beams.

"Why are you two hiding out in here?" one officer asked through his respirator in a husky voice.

"Working. What else?" Roger asked as he pointed aimlessly at the corner of the room. "These plowfucks left shit plugged in just about everywhere. Gotta check every nook and cranny."

Neither officer bothered to check in the direction that Roger pointed; clearly, they had more pressing concerns. "Did you see a woman come through?"

"Yeah, and a girl," Teddy answered. He jerked his thumb to the right.

"They panicked when they saw us and ran out front."

The officers sprinted off in the direction Teddy indicated, their breathing labored through their restrictive masks.

"That was too close," Roger said as he clutched his chest with one hand and wiped his forehead with the other.

Teddy waited a few seconds, then opened the door and stuck his head out. The records department appeared to be clear. Only the scattered trinkets of the dead occupied the countless cubicles. Teddy hurried back and opened the storage room as the little girl sneezed.

"Are they gone?" the woman whispered.

"They're gone, but you need to hurry before they circle back," Teddy said. He led the woman and the girl out of the room. "Sneak out the back—if it doesn't look safe, just hide and wait. I don't think these cops are going to search all night for you. Rest, if you can, and drink lots of water. You can beat this flu."

"I can't thank you enough," the woman said as fresh tears welled up in her eyes.

Her rheumy look reminded Teddy far too much of Jane's sobs during her final moments. For one brief second, he saw Jane in the stranger's face. Pain needled at his heart.

"Just go!" Teddy ordered curtly.

The woman and the child took off running and disappeared into the darkness.

"Took a gigantic risk," Roger said, studying his face.

"I'd do it again, if I had to."

"If they'd searched the room—"

"They didn't, though, did they?" Teddy asked sharply. "Besides, now those two have a chance."

"Nothing good lasts for long in this world anymore, hoss," Roger said with a frown.

"There has to be some good left out there," Teddy said. "Otherwise, what the fuck is the point of moving forward?"

"Maybe you're right," Roger said with a thin smile, but Teddy heard little conviction in his voice.

An old-fashioned air-raid siren went off, making Teddy jump.

"That's our cue," Roger said as he brushed past him, unperturbed. "Quitting time."

A voice shouted through a loudspeaker, "All civilian work details report back to your bus at once! You have five minutes!"

Roger whistled behind his paper mask as he sauntered out of the room. He kept the flashlight's failing beam pointed at the floor, taking care not to trip over the mess left behind. Teddy adjusted his mask and followed. He kept glancing uneasily over his shoulder, as if he expected to see the woman's face emerge out of the shadows.

"So, was this what you'd call a normal day?"

"You betcha. Aside from that little sideshow at the end, that is." He adjusted his sagging pants as he kept walking. "When we're outside clearing roads or digging ditches, we have to do some work, but it's easy-breezy when we're inside."

Teddy couldn't picture himself ever getting accustomed to it. As far as he was concerned, he wouldn't have to worry about it much longer either way. Once he found Ein, he still planned to escape. Although, the details of the yet-to-be-concocted heist weren't coming together in his head. They couldn't. He was too tired, too hungry, and too damn thirsty to do much thinking.

They left the records department and followed the others down the main corridor to the exit. A few FEMA officers stood against the wall with rifles across their chests, watching. The exit doors had rubber flaps covering them, and the walls were lined with sheets of plastic stapled in place. Faded CDC logos marked the worn plastic, which had many rips and holes that were sloppily patched with duct tape. A string of halogen lights dangled from the ceiling. People at the front of the line dropped their flashlights into waiting plastic crates and then raised their hands as they passed through the flaps.

"What's this about?" Teddy asked.

"Decontamination," Roger explained as he dumped his own flashlight and raised his hands over his head. "Get used to it. They do it every time we head back to camp."

"Don't see the cops going through the chemical carwash," Teddy muttered as he slowly brought his hands up.

"Double standards, hoss." Roger passed through the plastic flaps. "Remember not to—"

A nearby generator drowned out the rest of his advice.

"Not to what?" Teddy asked, unable to understand him.

He passed through the flaps and found himself in a makeshift plastic tunnel that led down to the courtyard. Two people wearing sealed, white biohazard suits stared at him through their mirrored visors. Both had chemical foggers attached to their backs and kept the device's nozzles pointed at Teddy.

"Move forward!" one of the white-suits ordered in a garbled voice through the speaker attached to his chest. "Arms up!"

Teddy kept walking and was inundated by a thick, white mist that burned his eyes and stole the air out of his lungs. He gasped and stumbled through the next set of flaps, snatching his mask off. Once outside, he came close to collapsing.

"You alright?" Roger asked.

Teddy placed his hands on his knees, wheezing as he slowly caught his breath.

Roger extended his hand, chuckling. "I told you not to breathe."

Teddy grasped his hand and pulled himself back up. "You didn't tell me shit," he said in a hoarse whisper.

"You just didn't listen. I'm thinking that's half of your problem." Roger shrugged and joined the others across the street and out in the courtyard, where he crumpled up his mask and tossed it into a waiting trash bin.

"My ears aren't the problem," Teddy said as he followed suit. "It's your accent. Nobody can understand that shit."

"You're one to talk," Roger said with a grin. "That Texas twang takes some getting used to." He looked over Teddy's shoulder and his grin vanished instantly. He turned his attention back to the road ahead and began marching away. "Just follow me. There isn't nothing to be done now."

Teddy coughed into the crook of his arm as he tried to keep up. "What are you babbling on about now?"

A drone buzzed low overhead, and Teddy followed it with his eyes to the street, where he realized what Roger must've seen. Teddy stopped walking, staring down the street in a dazed stupor. The other workers brushed past him, indifferently walking around him as if he was in their way.

Three idling prisoner transport wagons were crammed with frightened men, women, and children that Teddy assumed had been plucked from the building they were just in. Officers gathered around the back of the vehicles, stuffed a final few inside, and then locked the doors. More drones hovered overhead. What horrified Teddy, though, was unfolding further off in the distance.

Past the wagons, at the far end of the courtyard, stood a line of sick people, blindfolded, with their hands bound behind their backs. They coughed and hunched over, cowering in front of officers who remained invisible to them but stood with their weapons at the ready.

A fiery knot formed in Teddy's throat, and he felt tears of rage welling up in his eyes. "Those bastards. They can't do this. Those people didn't do anything!"

"Easy. Keep your voice down." Roger stopped and raised his hands to calm him down, as if he were a wild animal poised to strike. "I'm sorry. They normally do this somewhere out of view."

"I don't give a shit *where* they do it. This is wrong!" Teddy exclaimed.

His voice caught the attention of two officers idly chatting near the tunnel's exit.

"Is there a problem over here?" asked one of them, a young man with his gas mask tucked under his arm.

Teddy ignored the question and kept glaring at the execution line as if that was answer enough. The officer, annoyed, drew his truncheon and started advancing toward him.

"Teddy…" Roger said in an unsteady voice. "We have to go."

The other officers raised their rifles at the civilians and waited as two more people were led from around the side of the building. A woman and a young girl, both bound and gagged, were shoved into the sick crowd. Teddy's eyes widened—it was the same two he had tried to help not ten minutes earlier.

"No!"

The crack of automatic gunfire reverberated across the courtyard and sent crows fleeing their perches. The group of sick civilians jolted and then collapsed into lifeless heaps on the grass.

Teddy felt his muscles tense with a sudden rush of adrenaline. An overwhelming urge to run toward the group of executioners washed over him, but there was nothing he could do.

Roger grabbed him by the shoulder and shook him and his racing heart firmly. "Get yourself together, hoss."

"I asked if there was a problem here!" the officer with the truncheon snarled.

"None at all," Roger said with a smile. "My new coworker here is just getting orientated."

Teddy looked at Roger in a daze as his rational mind slowly emerged from seething fury's hazy delirium.

The officer stopped and lowered his weapon, shaking his head. "Then your coworker best orientate himself toward the bus before I bash his fucking head in!"

"Yes, sir," Roger said with a nod, leading Teddy away by his arm.

"I can walk," Teddy snapped as he tore free from Roger's grip. "I'm fine."

"You sure weren't fine back there." Roger frowned. "What the hell were you going to do? Take them all down with your bare hands?"

Teddy gave a heavy sigh. "I don't know what I was thinking. I just wasn't prepared to see that."

"Get used to it, sunshine. I already told you once—nothing good lasts for long in this world anymore."

Vue stood at the bus doors, waiting to collect the reflective vests and flashlights as the workers trickled back on. Parham stood nearby, his hooded gaze fixated on Teddy as if there was something aggravating him, but Teddy couldn't fathom what he could have done to make him so irate so quickly.

Teddy took off his vest and approached Vue, who warned him once more against idle chitchat while on the bus as he collected his vest. Normally he would've come up with a snarky response, but he didn't feel like talking and didn't think he'd be doing much of it on the ride back to camp, anyway. He lowered his head and trudged up the steps.

Salguero chuckled from the driver's seat when he saw Teddy. "Look at this cupcake's sour face," he announced to nobody in particular. "I was right—he won't last a week."

Roger tensed in front of him, probably expecting Teddy to react the way he always did. But Teddy didn't take the bait and kept moving. The men sat down, and after a few more minutes, the officers locked the security grille. The bus began heading away from Topeka.

During the long bus ride, everyone in the back was silent. Up front, Vue kept yammering on about some old television show, and Salguero reminisced about hunting deer back home in North Carolina. Occasionally, the sergeant cut in with tales of his sexual conquests, all of which sounded as fabricated as a Charles Dickens novel.

Teddy glanced out of his makeshift peephole only once. A shallow mass grave lay dug next to a rural Walmart's parking lot. Derelict trailers, abandoned excavators, and dump trucks surrounded the pit, which brimmed with skeletal corpses. He wondered if things would ever get better; he had witnessed enough death and despair to last ten lifetimes.

He kept his tired gaze on the seatback in front of him, though he felt Roger glance at him from time to time, likely wondering if he was okay. In truth, he wasn't. He was tired of death. He was tired of loss. All he could think about was saving Ein and getting the hell out of this awful place.

Maybe Roger could find some uneasy peace playing house with men who masqueraded as respectable officers for an agency that had stopped existing months ago, but Teddy sure as hell couldn't.

8

Teddy walked along the footpath between the dormitories. The crisp air had turned bone-chillingly cold as dusk approached and cleared out most of the residents who had loitered around the makeshift tent cities. Those who remained outside took refuge by steel drum fires, but the exhausted faces gathered around them looked strained, and conversation was sparse. There was also the odd strain of music drifting by, but for the most part, the only significant sound was the wintery wind whistling through the compound.

The bus had unloaded a long time ago, but Teddy's nose still hurt from Parham's blow earlier in the day. It was probably broken, but it didn't matter; he wasn't going to win any beauty contests anytime soon.

Roger had asked him to accompany him back to the dorm for another round of cards, but Teddy declined. He had a mission to complete, and it didn't include gin rummy. So, despite the weariness that had overtaken his aching body and the persistent throbbing of his wounded nose, he walked the footpaths for hours, looking for Ein.

Teddy found a few dormitory doors propped open and peeked inside during his search; Perry had not embellished his statement regarding the other dorms' cramped and dilapidated conditions. The walls were cluttered with clotheslines, Christmas lights, and an assortment of junk, while the bunks were piled high with broken trinkets and extra linens. The people inside didn't give him a passing glance, as they were too preoccupied with their newly formed cliques and seemed to cling to what remained of their family and loved ones. Ein wasn't anywhere in sight, and none of the people Teddy questioned recalled seeing a young guy with piercings and messy, purple hair.

If he were being honest with himself, Teddy would be the first to admit that he didn't know why he even gave a fuck. It wasn't like they had some special bond or a history beyond the stadium. Hell, Ein was essentially a stranger. But maybe what happened at the stadium was the reason for his obsession. He wanted to latch onto something, anything, after losing so much.

Teddy didn't know what drove him, and he didn't care. All he knew was that he wasn't leaving that camp without first finding Ein.

Eventually, hunger forced him to stop his search for the day and make his way to the dining hall. The chalkboard menu claimed the staff was serving chicken and greens. Instead, he got something that resembled pasta and white sauce. The pasta was chewy, and the sauce tasted like watery flour; just choking it down his gullet took a huge amount of effort. Others in the dining hall complained, but the officers in charge claimed that the chicken had expired, so they were forced to improvise.

Teddy observed an increase in the number of officers in the dining hall that evening compared to the morning. Most people wouldn't think twice about it, but the years he spent behind bars had altered his perception of these kinds of things. He figured that the administration expected more resistance from the people. However, Teddy knew it would take more than one bad meal to set them off. Unlike the prisoners he'd once known, most of the folks at the camp were soft.

After more fruitless searching in the frigid cold and on a stomach full of sickening food, he gave up.

I'll find you tomorrow, kid.

Teddy stuffed his hands into his pockets and headed to his dorm, defeated. Tension had settled between his shoulder blades, and his neck ached. The dorm's shower, which had seemed so disgusting to him last night, suddenly sounded appealing.

"Teddy!" a familiar voice called from the alleyway next to his dorm.

He turned and saw Roger sitting on a small crate beside a dying fire in a rusty steel oil drum.

"Sit down, hoss, and warm your hands for a bit!" Roger said jovially as he kicked a plastic milk crate out toward him. Teddy looked down at the crate and then over at the dorm with some slight hesitation, prompting a teasing, wrinkled grin out of Roger. "Unless you have some pressing dinner plans…"

"I already had whatever mess they were serving, so I reckon I'll sit and rest my bones for a bit," Teddy said with a shrug. He flipped the crate over and took a seat across from him. "I was just thinking about taking a shower."

"There aren't enough showers in the world to get that feeling off of you, son," Roger said sagely. "Dirt like that gets down deep."

Teddy was never one to speak metaphorically or wax poetic, but he agreed with Roger. He stretched his hands toward the fire; the warmth felt good and brought sensation back to his fingertips.

"Hell of a first day, wasn't it?" Roger asked as he studied him.

"Yeah…that's an understatement," he admitted as he turned his hands.

"I should've warned you about what they've been doing with the sick nowadays," Roger said regretfully. "Sometimes I forget how harsh things might seem to a newcomer."

"It's fine," Teddy said. "You didn't pull the trigger."

"No, but still," Roger said, choosing his words delicately. "Afterward, when we got back on the bus, the look on your face…something bad happened back at the stadium, didn't it? That's why you acted out." He paused and shook his head. "Whatever happened, I—"

"Please, stop," Teddy cut in curtly. A cascade of emotions was drowning him once more, and his frail state of mind just couldn't handle it. He stood up. "I don't want to talk about that right now—I can't."

"Okay," Roger said with a nod. "Just know, if you ever do…"

His voice trailed off, and he stared down into the fire in silence. The prospect of a shower momentarily forgotten, Teddy sat back down. He kept his head bowed and his hands extended toward the flames, fighting back tears.

A scruffy, mixed-breed dog crept out from around the other side of the barrel and looked up at Teddy with soulful brown eyes. It sniffed at his feet and then cautiously wagged its bushy tail. Teddy rubbed his face and regarded the dog with surprise.

"Don't mind Zoey," he said with a chuckle as he reached down and scratched the dog's back. "She's friendly and more than a little spoiled."

Zoey cocked her head to the side and perked her ears up. Teddy put a hand down in front of her nose. Zoey gave it a lick, and for the first time that day, Teddy had a genuine smile on his lips. Zoey barked happily and wagged her tail.

"Looks like she made another friend to mooch scraps off of!" Roger said as he laughed.

"She's a sweet dog," Teddy said as petted her. "How long have you had her?"

"Showed up about a month ago," Roger recalled. "Skinny little thing at first…I felt bad for her and gave her some food. She's been following me around since then and waits for me out here every morning."

Teddy scratched behind her ears. "The cops don't mind?" he asked as he glanced toward the tower.

"It's against the rules, but they don't say anything. Lots of folks here have pets. One cop—a gal named Walker—brings Zoey some meat out of the kitchen sometimes when she's on patrol."

"I guess they can't all be bad, right?"

"Not all of them, but most. Real soldiers and real cops would never do the things these people do," Roger said with sudden conviction. "I figure most of them used to be mall guards or some other wannabe before the flu wiped out nearly everybody. Then they got to fulfill their dreams. The real ones, the ones who actually believed in helping folks like us, either deserted or died. At least, that's what I think."

"I think so, too." Teddy went back to warming his hands, a little surprised by this glimpse into Roger's introspective mind.

"My grandpappy was in the army, so I know a thing or two about these things," Roger continued.

Teddy thought it best not to elaborate on his own experiences with law enforcement, but offered a thin smile. "Oh, yeah?"

"You betcha," Roger said proudly. "Those goons? He would've shot the whole damn lot of them. And Parham is a special kind of prick. You'd be smart to stay off his radar."

"I figure it's too late for that," Teddy said with a sigh as he ran a thumb over his busted nose.

"Yeah, I imagine so," Roger said, chuckled. "But, after tomorrow, you won't have to deal with him for two days."

"Why is that?"

"It'll be the weekend," Roger answered with a mocking smirk. "I guess our benevolent captors want us to fawn over the crumbs they give us."

"They're the best fascist leaders you could ask for," Teddy said. "Public executions on Friday, picnics in the park on Saturday."

Roger laughed, but Teddy's joke had soured his mood once more. Zoey walked back to Roger, wagging her tail, and flopped down at his feet.

"Either way, it's a nice little break. Maybe you can use the downtime to let that nose heal up," he suggested as he patted his four-legged friend.

"Doesn't sound like a bad idea," Teddy agreed. "So, what do you do with your free time around here?"

"Drink and gamble, mostly." Roger reached behind his crate and pulled out an old milk jug and two plastic cups. He popped the cap off the jug and filled one cup with an off-color liquid. "Drink this. After the day you've had, nobody could use this more."

"Hooch?" Teddy asked as he took the cup.

"Medicine," Roger corrected. "At least that's what my grandpappy called it."

Teddy smelled the strong ethanol content as he brought the cup to his lips. He hesitated and cocked a brow. "This Midwest moonshine of yours won't make me blind, will it?"

"If it does, you'll be too damn drunk to care!" Roger poured himself a cup and put the jug away, then smiled and raised his cup in the air for a toast. "Cheers!"

"Bottoms up," Teddy said with a shrug.

He quickly gulped the fiery liquid down; Roger tilted his head back and did the same. Both men lowered their cups and let out a loud belch. Zoey barked and then laid her head back down between her paws. They couldn't help but laugh.

"That's not bad," Teddy admitted in a hoarse voice before he winced and burped again.

"Thanks. I make it myself," Roger beamed. "Want some more?"

"No," Teddy answered quickly as he handed the cup back. "Thank you, though."

Roger took the cup and laughed. "So, aside from getting shitfaced with me, what else did you do this afternoon?"

Teddy leaned closer toward the fire. "I've been trying to find a friend."

"A friend, huh? All the working girls hang out near dorm twenty, but they ain't cheap and they ain't clean," Roger said with a grin, pouring himself another cup.

"Not that kind of friend," Teddy dully responded.

"I was just kidding, hoss," Roger said. "Didn't mean any offense."

"None taken. It's just been frustrating. I've walked this entire camp and there's no sign of him."

"What does this friend look like?"

"He's a skinny white kid with purple hair. In his twenties, I think. His name is Ein."

"Sounds like he'd be hard to miss in this crowd."

"You'd think so, but nobody I've asked has spotted him. Have you?"

"Can't say that I've met or seen an Ein—sorry." Roger tilted his head back and emptied the cup with a single swallow.

"Didn't think so…" Teddy stood up and rubbed his hands over the fire one last time. "Thanks for the drink."

Roger belched again, wiped his chin with his forearm, and struggled to put the cap back on the bottle. Teddy stuffed his hands in his pockets, turned, and started back toward the dorm.

Roger sighed heavily. "Hold up a second. I might be able to help."

Teddy paused and looked over his shoulder as a glimmer of hope flared in his chest.

"When's the last time you saw your friend?"

"Right after the train, we got separated. He went into one stall and I went into another."

Roger frowned. "I was afraid of that. That's when it always happens…" He stopped and reached down to pat Zoey. "I wouldn't waste too much time looking for him around here."

Teddy blinked, taken aback. "What the hell is that supposed to mean?"

"It means that he's not in any of the dorms," Roger explained with a solemn expression. "Knowing where he is won't help you, though, because you'll never get to him."

"Where?" Teddy asked as he took a step toward Roger.

"He's up in the administration building." Roger jerked a thumb toward the five-story building on top of the hill near the edge of camp.

"That doesn't make sense," Teddy said. "Why would they take him there?"

"I don't know," Roger admitted. "All I know is that anybody they take in there is never seen again." He paused and looked down into his empty cup. "Regular people like us can't get in there on our own. Maybe the red bands can come and go as they please, but not us."

Irrational anger bubbled inside of Teddy, inspired, he knew, partially by frustration and partially by liquor. "Come on! That's horseshit! Besides, how the hell would you know that?"

"You'd be surprised what the cops will tell you in exchange for some booze," Roger slurred. "I'm sorry, I really am, but your friend is gone."

"You're drunk."

"That doesn't mean I'm wrong."

Teddy waved a dismissive hand at Roger, turned, and stormed off toward the dorm.

"Hey, wait!" Roger called out as he held the bottle up in the air and waved it goofily.

Teddy ignored him and kept walking, even when he saw him nearly fall off his crate and send Zoey into a barking fit.

A shrill tone reverberated across the compound through the camp's PA system. Everyone who was gathered around the fires and gaming tables groaned, stood up, and started saying their farewells as the final hands were dealt and cigarettes were snuffed out.

"Nightly curfew starts in thirty minutes. All residents must return to their dormitories. Violators are subject to arrest and prosecution. Thank you for your cooperation."

As Teddy approached the dorm, his heart raced, and he felt heat radiating off his face. His hands trembled in his pockets, and he felt the thin veins along his neck protruding and pulsating. At first, Teddy thought he was just angry at Roger for spewing nonsense, but then he realized that it was something else entirely.

He was afraid that the man was right about Ein's fate. Teddy had searched the entire damn camp, so where else could the kid be? That building and the expensive-looking farmhouse he had spotted a mile or so past the fence were the only places left to look, and he doubted they would allow the kid room in some fancy manor.

Teddy looked over his shoulder at the building on the hill. At first glance, it was nothing special—just as plain and ordinary as any other structure there. However, the longer he stared at it, the more ominous it seemed to become.

Teddy looked away and continued to his dorm, thinking. The prospects of a quick escape were dwindling, and he felt himself become even more disillusioned with every step he took. Even worse, it felt like someone was picking away at his skull and tossing lit matches down his throat. Teddy massaged his left temple with one hand and placed his other against the door's sensor. The sensor flashed a green light as it recognized his chip.

"Sanders, Teddy—dorm twenty resident—access granted."

The door swung open, and Teddy staggered inside. The dormitory lights were dimmed, and the suspended ventilation shafts churned out air that was only slightly warmer than the wintry air outside. A handful of workers were already back and wrapped in blankets on their bunks, sleeping or burying their noses in books that they most likely stole from the empty offices they'd visited that day.

Teddy wandered toward his bunk while delicately rubbing his crooked nose and stretching his back. Whatever hooch Roger had concocted was more potent than he had expected it to be; his head swam and his vision was starting to blur. Nobody seemed to pay him any attention, but that suited him just fine.

He glanced at one of the communal showers and saw Perry with a hygiene kit tucked under his arm. Teddy was desperate for answers and figured Perry could provide some. He took off his jacket and threw it on his bunk, almost toppling over in the process. He turned and hurried after him, stumbling.

Perry stood at the washbasin, brushing his teeth, when Teddy walked in and stood next to him, placing a hand on the counter to maintain his balance. Perry leaned over the basin, spat, and rinsed his mouth in the running tap before looking over at Teddy.

"How was your first day?" he asked as he rinsed off his toothbrush. "You don't look so hot."

"I don't feel so hot."

"Then go sleep it off," Perry said. "I won't tell anybody you're drunk."

"Not until I ask you something."

Perry looked at him warily. "Ask."

"What goes on in that building?" Teddy asked in a slightly slurred voice.

"Which one?"

"The tall one at the front of camp."

Perry's expression fell flat, and he turned to the mirror once more. "I already told you it's an administrative building with a clinic."

"Yeah, I know what you said," Teddy replied, getting more and more aggravated by the second. "I want to know what goes on in the administrative side."

Perry carefully put his toothbrush in his kit and pulled out the dental floss. "How would I know? I'm not allowed in there."

Teddy leaned closer and narrowed his eyes. "I think you're lying to me."

"And I think you're drunk." Perry took some floss out of the dispenser and opened his mouth.

Teddy slapped the floss out of Perry's hands, grabbed him by his collar, spun him around, and pinned him against the basin. "Stop playing games! I want to know what goes on in there! They don't need five fucking floors for a bunch of paper pushers stapling forms together!"

Perry broke Teddy's grip and shoved him in the chest. Teddy stumbled back and faltered against the wall. Disoriented from the alcohol, he struggled to get back up.

"I don't know what goes on up there!" Perry exclaimed. "If I knew something, I'd tell you, okay? Sure, I've heard rumors, but that's all they are!"

"What rumors have you heard?" Teddy nearly pleaded in his rapidly deteriorating state even as he finally got back on his feet.

"I'm not in the business of repeating dangerous rumors," Perry snapped.

Teddy stared at him, perplexed, as his head swam. "Dangerous?" He held his hands out at his side and stumbled sideways. "How are rumors dangerous?"

"Fools that get caught jiving on about conspiracies end up on the hangman's noose."

"Why?" Teddy asked with his back against the wall to keep himself stable. "What are they afraid of?"

"Rabble-rousing. Rumors stir discord and rile people up—case in point." Perry shot him a disappointed scowl. "If I knew where your friend was, I'd tell you."

"Would you?"

"Why wouldn't I?"

"Well…" Teddy's voice trailed off as he gestured toward his red armband.

"Fuck you! Go on and spread nonsense, but don't look to me for pity when they take you away." Perry tucked the hygiene kit under the crook of his arm and stomped to the exit, but stopped in the doorway. "You're drunk, so I'm giving you a pass for what you pulled tonight. However, if you lay a hand on me again, it won't be the cops that you have to worry about. You feel me?"

Teddy stood in stunned silence. Clearly, he had underestimated the old man in more ways than one.

"Life isn't perfect in here, but it's a second chance," Perry continued. "The people running this place aren't perfect, but they're playing the best hand they can with the cards they were dealt. Why don't you try cutting them—and yourself—some slack?"

Perry without another word. Teddy, woozy, leaned against the wall and tried to regain his composure. After several minutes, he staggered out to the dorm. Perry had already disappeared to his bunk across the room from Teddy's. A wobbly Roger entered, along with a handful of others, right before curfew commenced.

Teddy lurched toward his bunk as he tried to sort through his mental fog. Despite Perry's assurances, what he had witnessed during his first day told him that the administration didn't give two shits about the civilians. Maybe Perry could convince himself that they were all acting for the greater good, but Teddy knew better. By then, he was almost certain that they had Ein locked away in the gray building, but the problem was that he hadn't the slightest clue about how to get inside.

Teddy flopped down on his bunk and rubbed his face in his hands, closing his eyes. It felt like the room was spinning. Before he dealt with anything else, he knew he needed to rest his eyes for a moment.

"Just rest 'em a little while," Teddy murmured to himself.

He rolled over onto his back with his arms over his head. In moments, he was fast asleep and snoring loudly.

9

NOVEMBER 26th, 7:05 A.M.

Orange sunlight filtered through thick, low clouds as a biting wind whistled through the camp. A thin layer of ice covered the rooftops and coated the tents and stalls in the alleyways. It was much colder than the day before, and many opted to stay inside instead of occupying the makeshift shops and gambling tables. The bazaars—clusters of haphazardly strung tents occupying some of the alleys—were mostly vacant.

Teddy walked along the footpath with his hands stuffed in his pockets and a woolen muffler wrapped around his throat and covering his mouth. He wasn't used to the cold, but was cognizant of the fact that winter's true savagery had yet to arrive.

Others milled past him, bundled up just as tightly in their jackets and blankets. They all seemed to speak in muted tones, and their conversations had a certain surreptitious undertone that hadn't been present the day before. A stark change in the atmosphere had happened overnight—a nearly palpable, nervous tension that seemed to pervade the very air itself. Most of the officers avoided the footpath and stuck to the catwalks that connected the guard towers, leering down below at the common folk.

Maybe people were starting to realize their own precarious predicament, and the government's façade as a shelter in the storm was chipping away like bad plaster. Still, Teddy didn't think the civilian population was much of a threat. He pegged the vast majority of them as weak, broken creatures who longed to feel safe again, even if it meant giving up their freedom. Sure, they were irritated, but they were unlikely to do anything other than bark and yelp like scrappy lapdogs.

He feared the officers' responses to any perceived hostility or aggression, especially since most of them appeared to be little more than trigger-happy rookies. Avoiding getting caught in the crossfire was his priority, making it crucial to leave sooner rather than later.

Teddy heard a hissing noise and smelled chemical vapors. He glanced to the side and saw two men hastily spray-painting something on one of the dormitories in an adjacent alleyway.

DON'T BE A SLAVE! RI—

Their creative pursuits were interrupted when one of the men saw him staring and alerted his friend. They dropped the cans and then darted away from the scene of the crime. Teddy continued on with the crowd toward the dining hall.

"Hey!" a voice called out from behind him.

Teddy turned at the sound and saw Roger coming toward him, with Zoey trotting happily at his side. She barked and ran ahead, tail wagging all the way.

Teddy crouched down, smiled, and patted her head. "You're a happy girl, aren't you?"

She licked his icy fingers and then sniffed his hand greedily. Once she realized he didn't have any treats to offer, her excitement ebbed, and she regarded him with reproachful eyes.

"Nah, she's just a furry mooch." Roger whistled at her and rubbed what was likely an aching forehead. "Come on, girl. Stop begging."

Zoey lowered her ears and then obediently turned back to Roger.

"I swear, she thinks the world revolves around her," he said, chuckled. His face was pale, and his eyes were bloodshot. He teasingly wagged a finger at her. "You're a mess, you know that?"

Zoey tilted her head at him and perked her ears up.

"I don't know. She looks better off than you do right now," Teddy said with a grin.

"I'm not arguing with that," Roger groaned. "My mouth is like sandpaper, and I feel like a truck ran over me."

"Drinking doesn't agree with you."

"Maybe, but I don't plan on quitting anytime soon," Roger replied defiantly, with a goofy smile. "How are you holding up this morning?"

"I'm fine."

"That's not good."

"How so?"

"That means that you didn't drink enough!" Roger slapped him on the back.

Teddy chuckled, turned, and continued walking down the footpath with Roger and Zoey. "I drank enough to make an ass out myself last night."

"That happens when good alcohol is involved. I don't remember much after you stormed off. Speaking of which, I, uh, didn't mean to piss you off. Being tactful was never one of my finer qualities."

"It's just frustrating—that's what this whole fucking situation is."

"I understand, hoss," Roger replied with a nod. "If you're worried that you made an ass out of yourself, don't think twice about it. I had no business flapping my lips."

"It had nothing to do with you," Teddy said. "When I went inside, I went off on Perry."

Roger raised a bushy brow. "Old Perry? The orderly?"

Teddy nodded. "I grabbed him and demanded to know more about that damn building you told me about. I was sloppy drunk and stupid…could hardly stand."

"How did that go?"

"About as well as can be expected," he said with a shrug. "He denied knowing anything and then scolded me about spreading rumors or something."

Roger laughed and shook his head ruefully. "Old motherfucking Perry…world-class liar and snitch."

"It seemed to me that he was telling the truth," Teddy said.

"Good liars always do." Roger spat on the ground. "He's a coward who wouldn't leave this place even if you paid him. If the fence ever fell down, he'd be the first one out there trying to put it back up. Never trust a collaborator."

Teddy chuckled until they turned a corner and found themselves on the main footpath leading past the gallows. Teddy noticed a fresh crop of corpses swaying in the wintery air. He took a few steps off the footpath to let everyone else by after he stopped.

Two officers posted in front of the gallows watched him and tightened their grips on their rifles. Teddy ignored them and studied each of the corpses. The burlap sacks rendered facial recognition futile, but he was confident he could identify Ein's lanky figure if it was suspended there.

"See him?" Roger asked as he joined him, Zoey on his heels.

"No," Teddy eventually said, the relief in his voice evident even in his own ears. "He's still out there somewhere."

They stared up at the victims for a few more moments before Zoey barked impatiently.

"Yeah, yeah, I'm going," Roger said as he reached down and patted her head. He stood back up and slapped Teddy on the back. "Let's go—old girl is hungry."

"We'd better grab something before they close it down," Teddy agreed.

"Not too excited for cabbage stew or whatever garbage they're serving. That's why here lately I've been on a liquid diet," Roger said cheekily.

"Judging by how bloodshot your eyes are, I'm not sure that's working out too well for you."

"Hey, whatever doesn't kill you, right?"

Teddy and Roger laughed as they walked past an officer who was on his way to relieve one of the men stationed at the gallows. Zoey still trotted beside them.

"Morning, officer," Roger told the man as he tipped an imaginary hat.

"I warned you before to get rid of that mutt," the officer said sternly as he stopped walking and glared down at the dog.

Zoey lowered her ears and growled softly.

"It's alright," Roger said as he stepped between them. He smiled at Zoey. "It's okay, girl. Calm down."

As if he'd spoken the magic words, Zoey stopped growling, rose to her haunches, and planted her front paws on his chest before wagging her tail and licking his face.

Roger chuckled and nudged her off. "Easy! Easy! You're embarrassing me!" Zoey barked happily and circled him once, still wagging her tail while she waited for her next command. Roger patted her and then gave her a gentle swat on the rump. "Get back to the alley and I'll bring you some scraps after work. Go on! Scooch!"

Zoey barked one last time and darted off, disappearing into the crowd. Roger chuckled and would have been back on his way to the dining hall, but was suddenly blocked by the officer's gloved hand.

"Dogs are illegal."

Roger beamed, reached into his jacket, and pulled out a small plastic bottle of off-color liquid. "Yeah, but so is hooch."

After giving Teddy an uneasy glance, the officer grabbed it, unscrewed the top, and took a whiff. Seemingly satisfied, he put the cap back on and allowed Roger to pass.

"Pleasure doing business with ya," Roger called over his shoulder.

"I don't want to see that mutt again," the officer halfheartedly warned.

Teddy followed Roger, but kept glancing back to make sure the officer wasn't following them.

"Are you sure it's wise to show your hand like that?" Teddy asked.

"They're not getting paid," Roger said dismissively. "Retention rate is horrible. Cops walk away from details just as often as civilians do. At the end of the day, they're working for food and the promise of a paycheck yet to come."

"Let me guess. Alcohol isn't something the government readily provides."

"Nope, but it helps me grease the wheels when I want someone to look the other way. A lot of them challenge you with some bullshit regulation just to see what you'll offer. I oblige them. Life is easier that way."

Teddy chuckled. How well Roger seemed to have adapted to the new way of life suggested that the man would've done well back at Tucson.

The crowd grew denser the closer they got to the dining hall, and Teddy fell silent as his mind wandered back to Ein.

It didn't take much for Roger to figure out what caused him to go quiet again. "I could be wrong about what I said last night. It's possible that he's not in that building. Could be in one of the dorms. Maybe you just missed him."

"Maybe."

"Your friend, uh, Dan, could be—"

"Ein," Teddy corrected.

"Ein, right—sorry," Roger said. "Ein could be out there looking for you, too."

Teddy offered him a thin smile and a faint nod, but said nothing else on the matter. Shouts echoed from up ahead, but neither of them paid it any mind.

Teddy scratched his arm over his coat where the chip was implanted, and an idea occurred to him. "Could one of your cop buddies find out where Ein is? They can look up the location of the tracking chips, right?"

"The ones up in the tower could, but I think it'll take more than a few bottles of shine to get them to tell me," Roger said. "If I still had some cigarettes, maybe, but I ran out a long time ago. I'm sorry, hoss."

"It's fine," Teddy said with a sigh. "I'll just keep looking after work."

"Even during a snowstorm?" Roger asked as he looked up at the clouds. "It looks like we'll be getting our first snow soon."

"That won't stop me," he said defiantly.

Roger chuckled. "I like your spirit, hoss. Heck, I ain't doing nothing tonight after work. I'll help you look. Maybe I'll turn Zoey into a bloodhound!"

"I appreciate it, Roger."

"Ain't nothing. I may have to bring some shine to keep me warm, though."

"Just keep that stuff away from me," Teddy said. "One cup had me seeing sideways."

"Too hard for you?" Roger asked with a mischievous grin.

"Apparently so."

"That's too bad. I guess I'll bring you a blankie and a juice box, then."

"Yeah…yeah." Teddy playfully punched Roger's arm. "Old, drunk bastard!"

"We'll work together to find him," Roger assured, nodding. "You betcha!"

The idea was appealing, but Teddy didn't think that they would find Ein unless they got into that administrative building.

The crowd on the footpath came to a stop; a large group was gathered at the dining hall's doors, jeering in frustration. Teddy and Roger stopped as those around them craned their necks and jostled each other, trying to see what was going on.

The dining hall doors were chained shut. A group of officers stood on the dining hall's roof, anxiously pointing their rifles at the crowd—particularly the people shouting profanities and thrusting their fists in the air. Mayville, his cheeks red from frostbite, stood behind the officers with a pistol in his trembling hand. As the civilians grew more clamorous, he cowered further back.

A recording boomed over the camp's PA system. "Community notice: due to a temporary inventory issue, contingency protocols have been implemented. Winter rationing is now in full effect. Return this evening for your daily meal."

A few of the more vociferous individuals started hurling small stones and handfuls of dirt against the front of the building; even in their anger, nobody dared directly antagonize the officers.

"…due to a temporary inventory issue, contingency protocols have been implemented. Winter rationing is now in full effect. Return this evening for your daily meal."

Some shouted a few more obscenities for good measure, but eventually obeyed the PA's commands. It was just as Teddy expected— a weak, broken population.

However, twenty or so stragglers continued to protest and insult the officers on the rooftop. For once, Teddy was unsure of what would happen next.

It looked like the officers were just as surprised at the show of defiance. They kept their rifles trained on the small crowd, but anxiously took a few steps back. Some looked over their shoulders at the sergeant and waited for his orders, but Mayville's eyes darted around as if desperately trying to find and pluck a solution out of thin air.

Feedback warbled from the loudspeakers that crowned the control tower erected at the center of the camp. Everyone fell silent as Hock's rough voice reverberated through the tower speakers.

"Civil disobedience will not be tolerated! Disperse and go to your work details at once, or I will authorize my men to use deadly force!"

The civilians gathered around the front of the building fell silent. Then, almost as one, they scattered like roaches. Evidently emboldened, the officers stepped to the edge of the roof and aimed their weapons at the workers as they scuttled away. Mayville relaxed and holstered his pistol with a smug grin.

"Come on," Roger said as he grabbed Teddy's shoulder. "Let's go before Gomer Pyle up there shoots an eye out."

Teddy frowned at the young sergeant, but followed Roger away from the dining hall. The mood was sour and tense; there was no more playful banter. In the wake of the almost-revolt, Teddy couldn't help but wonder if his initial assessment of the camp's population had been wrong.

Maybe now they're bent to the point of breaking.

10

Without breakfast, the bus ride was especially grueling. Teddy slouched against his window seat with a hand pressing down on his sour stomach. Acid bubbled inside and threatened to crawl up his esophagus. He felt slightly lightheaded.

Even worse, the heaters weren't emitting any warmth. All the passengers shivered with their arms crossed to trap whatever body heat they could. At the front of the bus, past the grille, Salguero manned the wheel, and Vue sat silently across from Parham.

A wiry, nervous-looking man with olive skin and jet-black hair sat next to Vue. He was wearing a white dress shirt, gray slacks, and scuffed dress shoes. A briefcase sat in his lap, and he anxiously fiddled with its handle as he stared down at the floor. Teddy thought he looked ridiculously out of place—like a college kid applying for his first job.

The sergeant announced back at camp that they were headed to some god-awful town about thirty miles away to get a power substation back online. The Topeka settlement was experiencing brownouts, and that just wouldn't do. Teddy didn't know much about electrical shit, so all he could do was hope he did not end up electrocuting himself.

He supposed that this was the reason they had a Middle Eastern man in ill-filling business casuals riding shotgun. If he had to guess, the man was some sort of engineer. People with knowledge like that had to be worth more than a whole truck full of food in this new world.

When Teddy boarded, he noticed a military Humvee idling behind the bus. A masked officer manned the gun turret and swept it menacingly over the crowd. Teddy didn't understand why they had an escort at first, but after seeing their travel companion, it wasn't too hard to put it all together.

If he listened closely, he could hear the Humvee's rumbling diesel engine trailing close behind the bus.

His mind wandered back to the day's task that awaited them at the substation. God, it was going to be a lot of work. Outside work. Cold work.

No gin rummy today.

Teddy was already hungry, tired, and so fucking cold; the prospect of forced labor only intensified his pain and discontent. Next to him, Roger looked just as miserable, and was quiet for once.

Whatever pitiful country road they were traveling on was in a state of extreme disrepair. Every pebble and crack in the sun-beaten asphalt made the bus rock on its axels. His window still had a small peephole scratched through the black paint, so Teddy kept peering outside. The landscape seemed to go on forever, with barren fields and lonely farmhouses with shutters closed, spanning as far as he could make out.

They rolled past weathered billboards, which he read with bored fascination. A couple of them announced the arrival of the Pratt County Harvest Festival, but Teddy figured that turned out to be a bust once the plague passed through. A few others proclaimed the salvation and mercy offered by Jesus Christ, but considering everything Teddy had witnessed, he doubted the truth of those advertisements as well.

One billboard caught his attention. Someone had scraped away the advertisement and replaced it with a sloppily painted message in red paint.

Join the Kansas Farmers Freedom Militia TODAY—tyrants and traitors not welcome.

Teddy wondered if these were the folks responsible for sabotaging the Topeka settlement. After all, it was only a matter of time before like-minded people gathered and imposed their own rules in the law's absence. There had to be hundreds of similar ragtag militias scattered throughout the United States fighting for dog-eared pieces of territory to call their own. Their motives were probably identical to those of the prison gangs Teddy knew of—power for the sake of power.

After passing the militia's billboard, he started noticing KFFM painted on the sides of some of the old barns and houses. A drawing of a skull and crossbones accompanied those letters across the side of an overturned semi-truck left on the road in a ditch.

It was pathetic, really, but was FEMA any better with its twisted ideology of rebuilding the same structure of government that had failed in the face of tragedy? Perhaps the good folks over at KFFM could do a better job. Hell, why not give a chance to the Yankee Doodle Dandy

Gang or whatever ridiculous names the other militias were going by? Teddy didn't care who sat on the throne. All he wanted was to get away from them all. He had never joined a gang back in prison, and he sure as hell didn't plan on joining one now that he was out.

Roger yawned and eyed him warily. "You're quieter than usual today."

Teddy looked away from the window and shrugged. "I could say the same about you."

Roger groaned as he cupped his forehead. "Hangovers and bumpy rides don't go well together. I was hoping for some eggs to soak up the booze in my belly, but no luck."

"I'm hungry, too," Teddy complained. "You wouldn't have a candy bar handy, would you?"

Roger chuckled. "All I brought is a deck of playing cards we won't get to use today."

Vue pounded his fist against the iron grille. "Yo! Shut up back there! No talking!"

Parham's attention snapped in their direction. He stood up abruptly and leaned his rifle against the bench before asking who was talking in a cold, stern voice and sliding his hand down to rest on his pistol.

Teddy was sure that the sergeant already knew. It was just an excuse for the man to posture.

Parham's gaze fixated on Teddy. "Who was talking?" he repeated, his eyes unwavering.

"Some idiots in the back," Vue responded passively as he waved a dismissive hand toward the grille.

"I wasn't asking you," Parham said without looking away from Teddy. "I was asking them—the cowards who refuse to speak up like men!"

Teddy rolled his eyes and went back to peering out of his peephole.

Parham became enraged upon seeing Teddy's nonchalance. "Open the grille!"

Vue looked up at him, evidently uncomfortable with the order. "Sir, we're moving. Rules say—"

"Fuck the rules!" Parham snarled, turning his rage on the officer. "If they try rushing us, shoot every one of them!"

Vue's eyes shifted from the sergeant to the passengers and then back again.

"I gave you an order!"

"Yes, sir." Vue slowly stood up, as if waiting for his superior to change his mind, and unlocked the grille.

Parham marched down the aisle to Teddy with his hand wrapped around the pistol's grip. He glowered at Teddy and growled, "Who spoke?"

Roger let out a heavy sigh and sat up, but Teddy reached an arm out to hold him in place.

"Why ask when you already know?" he asked.

Parham stopped and stood in front of Teddy's row. He puffed his chest out and stared down his nose at him. Clearly, his total lack of fear was unacceptable.

"Didn't my officer correct you yesterday?" he asked with narrowed eyes.

"I reckon so."

"Do you have a problem following rules?"

Teddy sized the short man up and decided he was unimpressed with what he saw. "Do you?" He jerked his chin in Vue's direction. "Your man told you not to come back here while the bus is moving. But fuck the rules, right?"

Tiny veins throbbed across the sergeant's neck, and his brown eyes widened. His entire face took on a wild, savage expression. The hand gripping the pistol shook. Teddy noted the man's control was slipping and decided it was best to submit and let him have his five minutes of glory instead of starting something he couldn't finish.

"I'm sorry that my words offended you, boss. I won't talk anymore."

As if Parham thought the words oozed with insincerity, or maybe was just trying to pick a fight no matter what, he quickly pulled his pistol from its holster and pointed it at Teddy's forehead. The other passengers gasped and cowered in their seats.

Roger's face paled. "Hey, my friend has a nasty habit of speaking off the cuff. Why don't we all just—?"

"Shut up!" Parham cut in. "Say another word and I'll put a bullet in you, too."

Roger went quiet. Teddy stared down the barrel of the pistol and willed himself not to flinch or even blink. He knew it was all bluster on the diminutive sergeant's end, and as soon as he calmed down, it would all be over.

Parham's brow twitched, and a humorless grin formed across his lips. The longer Teddy stared into the man's haunted eyes, the more he wondered if he had misjudged him. There was a hardness in them, a hatred, and it made him think that perhaps the sergeant was crazy enough to pull the trigger after all. Teddy went cold inside as he tried to read the man's face, but to no avail.

"Maybe I won't kill you," Parham mused. "But you'd be surprised what the human body can endure."

Instead of baiting the unstable man more than he already had, Teddy stayed silent.

"I can make your hard day of work especially taxing," the sergeant continued. He lowered the gun and pointed it at Teddy's right foot. "Have you ever stepped on a nail? I imagine this will feel like that, only a hell of a lot worse."

Teddy's heart raced as he eyeballed the pistol. He felt his body tense as he braced for the piercing, hot lead, but the sergeant finally saw what he wanted to see: raw, unbridled fear.

"Sad," Parham said with a humorless smile as he holstered the pistol. "You're not even worth a bullet, but if you test me again, I'll teach you the meaning of real pain."

As the sergeant turned and walked back down the aisle to the front of the bus, Teddy's body relaxed, although adrenaline still coursed through him. His heart was beating like a jackhammer, and his hands trembled.

Roger frowned at what was surely his pallid face. He reached a hand out and gave him a quick, reassuring pat on the knee, but Teddy couldn't even look at him. He was too ashamed at how he trembled like a coward. To stop his hands from shaking, he clenched his fists and turned to the window.

Suddenly, the bus was jolted by an incredibly powerful impact. All the windows on the left shattered, and everyone seated along those rows flew aside like ragdolls. Teddy's body was plastered to the window, and in the next instant, Roger was squashed up against him. Whatever it was, it continued pushing forward and scraped the crumpled vehicle across the asphalt for several agonizing seconds.

Rapid-fire shots reverberated from behind the bus as the Humvee's gunner started firing the .50 caliber, but whatever was shoving the bus continued unabated. With blood streaming down his lacerated face, Salguero clutched the dashboard radio mic with both hands.

"Transport to six-zero-nine to Jayhawk Control: we're under attack! Officers down! Need immediate—"

His words were cut short by a deafening cacophony of breaking glass, twisting metal, and horrified screams as the bus flipped and rolled off the country road.

Teddy flew out of his seat and flopped this way and that in the air as the bus rolled over and over. Flailing limbs and pieces of metal knocked against him until, in a dizzying fit of pain, he smacked into the roof and his world faded to black.

11

Sporadic pops of small-caliber gunfire sounded in the distance, but the din of heavier artillery was gone. As he came to, Teddy's ears rang, and excruciating pain raced up and down his back. The coppery taste of blood lingered in his mouth. Diesel fumes and exhaust hung heavy in the air, along with the tangy stench of gunpowder. He heard a few others around him groaning in agony and calling for help.

When he opened his eyes, he realized he was lying on his back with his arms stretched out above him. Each labored breath hurt, and his head swam. Just above him, he could see the warped remains of the bus seats.

Garbled, distant voices came out of the dashboard radio. "Break, Jayhawk Control to—"

Static swallowed the voice coming from the speaker as Teddy forced himself to sit up, sending a fresh wave of pain crashing through his body. At the front of the bus, past the remnants of the security grille, the radio mic swung like a pendulum from the overhead dash. The windshield was shattered, crushed down to a narrow slit, and the doors bowed inward. Hydraulic fluid spritzed from the door mechanism onto Sal's severed leg, which hung crushed between the frame and the dash. What remained of him was pressed against one side of the security grille by an axle that had punched through the floorboard.

Vue lay upside down against the side of the bus, his head bent behind his shoulders and both arms twisted in opposite directions; an image of a destructive toddler going to town on his playthings came to Teddy's mind. The visiting man hadn't been thrown too far away from him, and lay dead with a sliver of glass sticking out of his throat. Parham wasn't anywhere in sight.

The jarring scene froze Teddy in place for a moment as he sat on the

91

floor, his mouth agape. A few other passengers around him shoved the dead off of them and rose to their feet, cursing and crying out in pain.

Automatic gunfire rang out from the field nearby, and bullets peppered the side of the vehicle faster than any of them could blink. The gunner cut a merciless straight line across the length of the bus. Bullets ricocheted madly, and what little glass was left exploded into tiny shards. The passengers who were standing were quickly cut down as the lead tore through their bodies. Teddy ducked and covered his head, squeezing his eyes shut as bullets whistled by.

After a few moments, the gunfire stopped, and the bullet-riddled corpses swayed drunkenly before collapsing.

Roger.

Teddy crawled over the dead on his hands and knees, searching for the only friend he had made at the camp. He kept a low profile, making sure to stay beneath the windows and unnoticed.

"Roger!" he called, his voice harsh and raw.

A gnarled, gory hand reached out from under one of the bodies and grabbed his ankle.

"Help me…" a woman's raspy voice begged.

Teddy tore his ankle free from her weak grasp and continued crawling, searching. Liquid dribbled from the ceiling, and the vehicle's engine gave a few final clunks before it, too, expired. He was freezing. His clothes were getting soaked with diesel fuel. *Everything* was saturated with it. He had to get out; the whole bus was a powder keg waiting to blow.

"Roger!" he called again, more frantic this time.

Finally, not too far away from the grille, he spotted him. Roger lay impaled by one of the frame's steel support beams. He tried to pull him off the gore-slathered steel, but his body wouldn't give. Besides, Roger's skin was already cool to the touch; Teddy knew it was too late.

He was dead.

Teddy passed a hand over the man's eyelids to close them, but it turned out he couldn't even manage that. One of Roger's eyelids remained open, and the other only closed halfway. It left him with an unsavory postmortem wink instead of the appearance of eternal rest.

Teddy stared at him for a few seconds, struggling to maintain his composure.

A second burst of automatic gunfire ricocheted off of the back of the bus and struck down another passenger who had managed to get to her feet. Teddy snapped back to his current predicament like a whip. He had to find some way out.

The front end of the bus was crumpled and impassable. Teddy turned toward the rear and noticed that the welded seals that once held the emergency exit shut had broken off during the accident. The door stood ajar and flapped lazily in the chilly wind.

Teddy started crawling toward it as panic tightened its grip. Whoever attacked the bus was more than likely watching that damn door and would shoot as soon as anybody stepped out. Yet, if he stayed behind, he'd either burn up or get popped off when the attacker came by to pick through the remains. All he could do was hope that whoever was out there was a bad shot.

Teddy tumbled out onto the grass embankment. The machine gun's response was immediate, but sloppy; whoever was manning it probably didn't think any of the passengers were still alive and weren't prepared for anyone to escape. Bullets thwacked against the swinging door and pitched dirt up into the air as errant rounds struck the ground.

Teddy scrambled up the embankment as bullets whizzed by. Shards of glass embedded deep in his palms, and the diesel fuel burned as it seeped over and into his wounds. He forced himself to push past the intense pain and scurried on like a madman.

Once on the asphalt, he rolled over to take cover on the opposite side of the overturned bus and pressed his back against it. Several more bullets hit the bus at random, and then the shooting stopped. As he caught his breath, he peered around through wary eyes, expecting to see some masked gunman ready to unload on him, but he saw no one. He was safe—if only temporarily.

To Teddy's right, he saw what had pushed the bus off of the road. A bulldozer with a maligned bucket loader idled in the middle of the road amongst a sea of shattered glass and pieces of steel paneling. It had comically sharp teeth spray-painted across the front, and had left muddy tracks across the road from an overturned grain silo, where it must have been lying in wait for its next victim. The corpse of a grizzly white man wearing military fatigues was still seated in the cab; he had been shot in the head. Teddy could just make out some homemade insignias and KFFM in place of where the US Army patch would've normally been on his uniform.

Teddy tried to stand, but his right leg was numb. Confused, he looked down and noticed a crimson blossom forming in the middle of his thigh. His diesel-soaked denim gave the blood an oily sheen.

I've been shot.

Whatever numbing effects the adrenaline had had were wearing off, and intense pain radiated up his leg and all the way to his core.

"Just what I needed," Teddy grumbled between his clenched teeth as he scowled and forced himself to his feet.

Brass shell casings lay everywhere at his feet. Teddy glanced around the rear of the bulldozer and rested an arm against it to catch his breath and take his weight off his injured leg. Across the street, three pickup trucks with oversize tires were parked in a line, about one hundred yards away in a frozen field of corn. The truck in the center of the convoy had a machine gun mounted on its bed, which was manned by a bald, white man with flabby arms. The fat gunner kept his weapon pointed at the bus, his face contorted in a wide, manic grin. Six others, all men, crouched among the dead stalks between the pickups, armed with hunting rifles and a few shotguns. They wore an odd hodgepodge of army uniforms and woolen winter gear.

Proud members of the local militia?

A few yards ahead of the bus, Teddy spotted the rear of the Humvee that had escorted them. The vehicle's armored paneling was severely damaged, with the plates barely clinging to the frame. Thin tendrils of smoke rose from the engine, and the remnants of the passenger side door, along with shards of glass, littered the asphalt. The machine gun's barrage had practically eviscerated the officer who had manned the gun turret on the roof. His gory remains draped over the weapon, the smoking barrel of which was still pointed skyward.

Parham, his face bloodied and his left eye swollen shut, had taken cover on the opposite side of the vehicle and held a pistol in his hands. One of the surviving officers from the Humvee, a young man who looked fresh out of high school, sat next to him with a rifle. His whole body trembled, and his blue eyes stared ahead, unblinking and unseeing. Two other officers were sprawled out in pools of blood on the asphalt with their spent weapons nearby.

Parham's gaze met Teddy's, and the sergeant pointed his weapon at him as he hissed, "Stay back!"

The damn fool was more concerned about a wounded civilian than he was about the demented rednecks shooting at them.

"Relax!" Teddy shouted back. "I'm not after you, and I'm not trying to escape! I'm shot!" He removed his bloodstained hand from his thigh and held it up as evidence. "See?"

Parham hesitated a moment before lowering the pistol and holding it against his chest once more. "Backup is on the way. Just got to hold them off a little longer!"

The young officer fidgeted and started to visibly hyperventilate. His knuckles turned white as he gripped the rifle harder.

"Stay calm, corporal!" Parham ordered. "Stay low! Blow their goddamn heads off if they break our cover!"

The corporal nodded as his face blanched.

One of the militiamen keyed a megaphone; feedback squawked from across the field. "Attention, tyrants: y'all trespassing on sovereign land! Quit yer hidin' and come on out! We done caught ya!"

The frightened corporal's eyes darted toward the no-man's-land as if he were seriously considering it.

"They'll kill you without hesitation," Parham said coldly.

After a few tense seconds, the militia gunner unleashed another volley of gunfire. Bullets peppered the side of the overturned bus, punching through it as if it were made of cheesecloth. Sparks flew wildly as lead scraped against iron. Finally, the diesel fuel caught, and flames engulfed the bus. The inferno blasted a forceful wave of heat in all directions. The gunner ceased firing, and the militiamen cackled and cheered at the sight of the fiery explosion.

Teddy was shoved from his hiding spot as the blast hit him in the back. He landed on hands and knees on the asphalt between the bulldozer and the disabled Humvee. It took less than a second to realize his exposure, and only another for the militiamen to halt their hooting and hollering and open fire, treating him like their very own sitting duck. Bullets whizzed past as he dragged himself toward the Humvee. His maimed right leg scraped across the ground, leaving a bloody streak, but he didn't slow down. Fear did a fine job of dulling the persistent pain of his wound.

A burst of scattered buckshot ricocheted off the ground nearby, and some pellets sliced through his skin. Teddy howled but kept pushing until he could roll over and take cover between Parham and the young corporal. He pressed his back against the vehicle and clutched his injured thigh with both hands, wheezing under the strain.

The gunfire stopped, and the megaphone crackled to life again, "I'll make y'all a deal. Whoever throws down their weapon and comes on out can live to see tomorrow!"

"Fuck you!" Parham shouted. "If you want our weapons, come and take them!"

Teddy heard the militiamen laugh, and the one holding the megaphone continued. "Offer still stands for the others! You have five seconds to think!"

The corporal looked at Teddy and then at the sergeant, whose bottom lip quivered.

"Don't," Parham said sternly.

"I-I-I'm not a soldier," the corporal stammered. "I was just a cadet in the police academy when the flu hit, and the feds scooped me up. I never signed up for any of this." He slowly rose to his feet. "I'm sorry."

The corporal picked up his rifle and limped out into the open, waving a hand in the air.

"Coward! Get back here!" Parham shouted, but the corporal ignored him.

"Don't shoot!" the corporal pleaded as he dropped his rifle on the ground at his feet. "I surrender!"

The corporal's body danced a sordid jig as a barrage of bullets ripped through him. After a few seconds, the gunfire ceased, and he collapsed in a bloody heap. Uproarious laughter erupted from the band of militiamen.

Parham and Teddy exchanged an uneasy glance—they both knew what was coming. Sure enough, the dead corn stalks rustled as the militiaman advanced toward their position.

"Backup is on the way," Parham assured him again.

"Yeah? So are those rednecks," Teddy said. "We need to go."

Parham sighed and glanced down at his ankle. Teddy followed his gaze and noticed for the first time that the sergeant's right foot was twisted, and bone protruded from his pants. Dark blood pooled around him, and Teddy could tell that he was a minute or less away from passing out.

"I'm pretty busted up," Parham said woozily. "If you run, I won't stop you. Hide behind that silo across the street, and you'll probably be safe."

"And you?" Teddy asked.

"I'm not going anywhere," the sergeant responded flatly, staring down at the gun in his hands. "I'll hold them off."

"You'll die."

"I'm dead either way," he said as he motioned to his fractured leg. "Either by their bullets or by bleeding out."

"But you—"

"Go before I change my mind!" Parham growled. "Hide!"

Escape was tempting, but he had to get back to the camp; Ein was still stuck inside somewhere. Besides, he had never run from a fight before; he sure as hell wasn't going to let a bunch of militant farmers make him start.

Teddy looked at the Humvee. It was his only chance.

He reached up and grabbed the driver's side door handle and pulled himself up, biting his lip to keep from screaming.

"The engine's shot to hell," the sergeant said in a disheartened tone.

"You're wasting your time."

Teddy ignored him and peered through the door's broken window. A bullet-riddled officer sat in the driver's seat, his head hanging out the window. His dead eyes had rolled up in their sockets to gaze upward. Two more corpses slumped over in the back. Legs dangled down in the middle of the Humvee from the turret nest. The gunner had attempted to crawl out but was too slow.

The sound of the militiamen trudging through the corn grew closer. Teddy opened the driver's side door, pulled the officer out, and let him flop to the ground. The corpse landed next to the sergeant like a sack of potatoes.

Parham winced. "What are you doing? I told you the motor's shot! It's not moving!"

Teddy ignored both the sergeant's shouts and his body's painful protests. He crawled toward the center of the vehicle, grabbed the gunner by his legs, and yanked him down. The corpse slumped through the hole, landing with a thud and splattering gore across the floor. Teddy wiped blood off his face and climbed up the steel rungs. Growing up in Texas, he knew guns well.

Once in the turret's nest, Teddy grabbed the .50 caliber's handle grips and aimed down at the field. A row of six militiamen stood only fifteen yards from the road, and each one froze at the sight of Teddy pointing his weapon at them. Fear washed over their faces—they clearly hadn't expected anyone to be in fighting condition, let alone daring enough to emerge after what they did to the officer who tried to surrender.

As shock gave way, the militiamen hoisted their hunting rifles and shotguns to their shoulders, but Teddy was quicker. Four of them were knocked back as the large rounds punched baseball-sized holes through their bodies. The remaining two scuttled off on all fours, taking cover in the flattened corn, as Teddy fired relentlessly. Chunks of earth and broken stalks flew up as the rounds tore up the ground around them. One man's head exploded like a rotten pumpkin.

The final militiaman lost his nerve, dropping his weapon and sprinting toward the trucks. At the center truck, the fat man scrambled out of the cab and clawed his way into the elevated bed where the machine gun was welded down. Teddy trained his weapon on the gunner before he could open fire. The pickup bucked and rocked as rounds tore through it, the driver's blood splattering the dashboard and streaking the windshield. The fat gunner, caught off guard, was pummeled by rounds that tore into his gut and crushed his chest. His plump lips formed an O as blood surged out of him.

Teddy continued firing at the truck, fearing someone else might climb into the bed and take the fallen gunner's place. After several more shots, the engine block was thoroughly destroyed. Suddenly, something ignited, and the truck erupted into a massive fireball.

His palms bled, and his arms went numb; the gun's recoil was brutal, even anchored to the Humvee. Spent brass casings scattered and cordite stung his face. He wanted to turn the weapon on the other two trucks, but his vision blurred, and his legs collapsed as soon as he paused his assault.

Exhausted, Teddy let go of the guns and slumped back against the turret's rail. He'd lost too much blood and was on the verge of passing out. As his consciousness faded, he watched the two remaining pickup trucks speed away, leaving behind the burning wreck of the gunner's rig and their dead scattered across the ravaged cornfield.

12

Hours later, Teddy awoke in an unfamiliar bed in an unfamiliar room.

A pale blue paint covered the windowless walls, and harsh fluorescent bulbs illuminated everything in cold, clinical light. The potent stench of chemical disinfectant hung in the air and seemed to stick to the inside of his nostrils. On one wall, a framed poster hung next to a medical chart depicting the human skeletal system.

His eyes lingered on the poster as his vision went in and out of focus. The poster displayed a pale man wearing a surgical mask, with text overlaid across the entire width of the image.

KNOW THE SIGNS—STAY ALIVE!

Cough? Fever? Body aches? Report it!

Early detection and medical intervention can save your life!

Teddy scoffed—he knew exactly how far early detection and intervention had gotten folks. He groaned and tried to raise his head, but it felt unusually heavy. There was a strange metallic taste in his mouth, and he felt lightheaded, as if he had been drinking. The pulsing, gut-wrenching pain he had experienced earlier had been reduced to an insignificant throbbing.

I've been drugged.

They replaced Teddy's clothes with a flimsy, white gown, and he lay on a gurney with its steel rails pulled up to keep him from rolling over and onto the floor. An IV fed into his left forearm. Wires and probes were attached to his skin, connecting him to monitors on a cart nearby.

No, not drugged—sedated.

His eyes found a door along the wall nearest his feet. Teddy tried to move, but the drugs made it so he could only squirm weakly on the bed. After struggling against the sedatives for a few minutes, he was exhausted. He closed his eyes and lay still.

"I was wondering when you'd wake up," a voice said from the corner of the room. "I wasn't sure how much shit they pumped into your system."

Teddy's eyes snapped open, and he turned his head toward the voice. Hock sat in a recliner positioned next to a small side table in the corner. He still wore his dress uniform, but his face looked troubled, as if his mind was elsewhere. An unlit cigar hung out of his mouth, and he idly flicked open his lighter and then thumbed it closed again.

"The man from the train," Teddy rasped.

"Keep running into each other, don't we?"

"What do you want?" Teddy asked, frowning. "Where am I?"

Hock stood and stretched. He slowly walked toward the bed, still flicking his lighter. He stared down at Teddy, as if mulling over his response.

"They said you took quite a blow," he said, ignoring both of Teddy's questions. "You lost a lot of blood."

The lieutenant walked around Teddy's bed and then stopped next to his bandaged leg.

"What do you want?" Teddy asked again.

Hock flicked open his lighter, spun the spark wheel, and held the flame just below his cigar. He methodically rolled the cigar between his fingers until the tip glowed orange. As he took a few initial puffs and put the lighter away, Teddy grew irritated with the man's deliberate lack of answers.

Hock took his first drag, savoring it like a sommelier with a vintage bottle of wine. As he blew the smoke toward the ceiling, he smiled. The cloying smell of the cigar filled the room, making Teddy cough.

"Tell me what you want!"

"Do you think they're making Churchills anymore?" Hock asked.

Teddy was taken aback by the nonsensical question. "What?"

"Churchills." Hock took the cigar out of his mouth and held it out to Teddy, once again rolling it between his fingers. "If you get the right brand, then they have a woody flavor that hits the pallet just right." He put the cigar back in his mouth. "Do you smoke, Mr. Sanders?"

"No."

"Pity," the lieutenant said. He blew another puff of smoke up at the ceiling. "I'd wager it's too late for you to enjoy one of life's most heavenly vices. I don't believe anybody is making Churchills anymore."

"No, I reckon not," he answered flatly, waving a hand in front of his face to clear away the smoke.

"I reckon not," Hock repeated. "Fine cigars are in very short supply. I only have three left. Can you believe that? Only three left…"

Teddy's vision floated in and out of focus as he stared up at the lieutenant, cupping a hand over his strained eyes. "Is there a point to your rambling?"

"I'd trade most of my paltry army of meritless milksops for a box of cigars," Hock snapped. "You see, Mr. Sanders, most of the men and women under my command are inexperienced cowards, although there are a few who stand out. Despite the horrible hand God has dealt me, there are a few cards worth holding. Parham, as obnoxious as he can be, is one of my better sergeants. He's admittedly crass, but he keeps the slobs under him in line." Teddy lowered his hand as Hock took another drag of his cigar. "When the bus was attacked, two civilians from your detail escaped, but you stayed behind and did something you didn't have to do."

"What happened to them?"

"To whom?"

"The two who escaped."

"They were chipped, so we tracked them down and executed them. But they're of no consequence." He waved his hand dismissively. "What matters is that, thanks to you, I still have one of my best men."

"I didn't do anything for him," Teddy curtly replied. "I was just protecting my ass."

Hock smiled passively. "Perhaps, but I don't think that matters. What matters is that you have grit."

"Grit?"

"Courage, mettle, fortitude," the lieutenant elaborated. "Whatever you want to call it, you showed that you have it. Blood is a precious resource, and I would have never given you so many liters of it if I didn't see your true potential. Any other civilian would've been one more body for the pit."

"I was just doing what needed to be done."

"Exactly." Hock blew another puff of smoke toward the ceiling and then knowingly waggled a finger at him. "It appears that I misjudged you on the train."

"Why are you telling me this?" Teddy asked.

"I came here to do more than just thank you," Hock answered as he rolled the cigar between his calloused fingers. "You see, circumstances are forcing me to recruit from the camp's population."

"What sort of circumstances?"

Hock simply took another puff and then blew the smoke up and away.

"I want you out of that work crew and in a uniform. I need someone like you."

Teddy was awestruck by the unexpected proposal. Having spent so many years on the wrong side of iron bars, he never would have imagined becoming someone who held the keys—nor did he find this proposal particularly appealing. The lieutenant's offer was a nonstarter. How could he work with the likes of Parham? His temper would only get him a spot on the gallows.

Hock studied Teddy's expression as if he were trying to read a difficult textbook. He gave up and sighed. Thick ashes hung off the tip of his cigar. "Unfortunately, the doctor wants to spend some time with you after you heal up, so I can't take you yet."

"What doctor?" Teddy asked, confused by the turn the conversation had taken.

Hock took his cigar and tipped the ashes toward Teddy's bandaged leg. "When he's finished doing whatever the hell he does down there and releases you back into my custody, we'll circle back to this."

Teddy's brow furrowed. "What the hell are you talking about?"

Before the lieutenant could answer, the door opened and a male nurse wearing blue scrubs entered with a medicine cart. The nurse appeared surprised at the sight of the lieutenant and came to an abrupt stop.

"Sir…" He gave a nervous salute. "The doctor told me to administer some more hydromorphone. I didn't mean to interrupt."

"I was just leaving," Hock said. "Go about your business."

He walked toward the door, puffing his cigar. The nurse held up a shaky finger.

"Um, sir, you, uh, can't smoke in here," he said awkwardly. "It's, uh, clinic rules."

The lieutenant paused and cocked a brow at the young man. He took a long drag and blew smoke into the man's face with a grin. "I won't tell if you don't."

"Asshole," the nurse muttered under his breath once Hock was gone and pushed the cart to Teddy's bed.

As he brought out a small vial and a syringe, then began fiddling with the IV port, Teddy said, "I need to speak to the doctor."

The nurse ignored him and pushed the syringe's plunger.

"Are you deaf?" Teddy asked angrily as his ears started ringing. "I said that I need to…speak…to…"

"Sweet dreams," the nurse said as he withdrew the spent syringe from the port and tossed it into a red bin on his cart.

Within seconds, Teddy's world started spinning. Then he drifted off into a deep, drug-induced slumber.

13

NOVEMBER 27th, 2:07 A.M.

Mark Hammond awoke to the sound of gunfire.

He lifted his head off his desk and looked around the darkened study, feeling hungover and delirious. The stubble on his cheeks had grown into a thin, patchy beard. He knew from looking in the mirror the day before that his wrinkled face and the whites of his eyes were yellowed with jaundice as his failing liver struggled to keep up with his relentless drinking.

Restful sleep remained elusive and was a luxury he hadn't experienced in a very long time. Each time he attempted to sleep, the same nightmare played over and over in his mind.

Laura, pale and deathly sick, staring up at him. The soft, supple pillow as he pressed it down on her face. Her nails digging into his forearms and her legs flailing as she clung to whatever life she had left. The feeling of her body going limp as she succumbed.

Hammond's bouts of dreamless rest only came from the bottle, and at the expense of his rapidly declining health. Empty whiskey bottles covered his desk and littered the floor. The air was sour with the stench of old urine and spilled alcohol, but his nose had already become accustomed to it. Hammond smacked his dry, cracked lips and stared at the empty glass on his desk. He frowned and reached for the bottle he knew was tucked away in his desk drawer, but stopped when he remembered he was already down to his last few; he didn't think they'd bother restocking his personal supply anytime soon.

Won't be too much longer until I'll be making rancid moonshine in my goddamn bathtub.

Who was he kidding, though? He'd happily drink moonshine, rubbing alcohol, or anything else that took his mind off the pain, even if only for a little bit.

He withdrew his hand, and his heavy eyelids shut once again.

Then he heard more gunfire—closer this time. Hammond's eyes shot open, and he forced himself to stand. He tied his soiled robe and shuffled to the study window with one hand pressed against his aching lower back.

On the moonlit ground below, a black Chevrolet Suburban with flashing blue police lights flashing had rammed through a section of the fence and wildly wove along the road. Its front end was buckled, and the driver's side front tire had blown. Two more SUVs sped out of the vehicular sally port and gave chase. Officers manning the perimeter guard towers fired at the erratic vehicle as it veered off the road and tried to disappear into a dead cornfield. Searchlights came to life and focused their beams on the fleeing SUV. Men wearing what looked like FEMA uniforms looked out from the shattered rear window and fired at their pursuers, but to little effect.

In an instant, and under a steady rain of lead, the fleeing SUV lost one of its rear tires. It careened to the left, rolled over three times, and came to a smoldering stop on its back in the middle of the field. The pursuing vehicles skidded to a stop behind it. Bloodied, injured officers crawled out of the wrecked SUV and tried to run, but none of them made it very far.

Deserters, Hammond surmised. It didn't surprise him; the ramifications of announcing emergency rationing had undoubtedly put people on edge. He was quite certain that the back of that overturned SUV contained MREs and ammunition.

They couldn't be the only ones. He figured many of Hock's men were dipping their hands in the cookie jar to build themselves a nice little stockpile. They probably overlooked the fact that needless theft and hoarding would only exacerbate the situation. He even noticed that some of his own security team seemed to have vanished during the day.

Hammond trudged back to his desk, ignoring the sporadic pop of gunfire that persisted from somewhere outside. He plopped down in his chair with a heavy sigh, and his eyes shifted toward the reassignment packet that sat on his desk.

"Three years…"

How was he supposed to manage a camp for three years when he already knew it wouldn't last through the summer?

He picked up the empty glass and held it in front of his face, slowly tilting it from side to side and watching as the moonlight made it almost glitter. In his distorted reflection, he saw the face of a stranger. He looked like a goddamn ghoul. Then again, after what he did to Laura, wasn't that an accurate description?

Disgusted and haunted by his own appearance, he tossed the glass over his shoulder as the memories overwhelmed him once again. Hammond reached down with a shaky hand, opened his desk drawer, and peered down at his last bottle of whiskey. Moonlight caught on a metal object next to the alcohol. His tired eyes lingered on the old revolver with the marbled grip.

The bottle or the gun—his hand hovered over them as he considered his options. One would offer him a temporary reprieve, while the other would silence the ugliness forever.

Mark Hammond chose the latter.

14

DECEMBER 17th

One hundred and ten tiles adorned the ceiling.

Teddy knew that because he'd counted every tile at least five times every day during his brief periods of lucidity. Time itself seemed to have an abstract quality, as hours morphed into days. How many days had passed since he was admitted? He hadn't a clue.

After the meeting with Hock, they had rolled his bed into a different, smaller room while he was asleep. The walls were painted the same tepid blue as before, but they appeared to have been made from some sort of sealed concrete. They replaced his bedside monitor with an even more advanced version that invaded his body with more tubes and wires. There were no chairs in the room, nor posters on the wall, but there were two security cameras mounted in opposite corners of the ceiling.

Another drastic change was the door itself. Instead of a regular hospital room door, Teddy's door was made of a solid piece of steel, resembling a ship's bulkhead entrance. It seemed to operate remotely by whoever was watching the cameras and made a loud hissing sound each time it opened. He also knew that the room was pressurized, because every time the door opened, his ears popped.

Nurses clad in blue protective suits and hooded respirators came and went sporadically. The pain medication clouded his sense of time, making it difficult to discern any pattern in their visits. The few who appeared during his lucid moments moved stiffly and without emotion, performing their duties like automatons.

Bandages changed? Check. Bedpan emptied? Check. Vitals taken? Check. Medication administered? Check.

They never spoke to him or answered any of his questions.

It was maddening, but the truth was that Teddy was afraid that his fragile grip on reality was slipping away. He figured it wouldn't be much longer before he'd be no different from any other babbling lunatic in an asylum.

He didn't know why he was being kept in that room, and he didn't know why the nurses wore those blue-suits. It genuinely scared the shit out of him, because he didn't feel sick—just doped up and very much like a prisoner in his own flesh. Until he regained some strength, he was powerless and at the mercy of their needles.

His legs tingled and sensation started to slowly return, but all he could do was hope that he would have enough strength to make a move before another blue-suited asshole sedated him again. Their timing had been better than his thus far.

Teddy stared up at the ceiling and started mentally ticking off tiles as he waited to see if his body would finally cooperate. But, after he counted all the tiles twice and was about to start on round three, the door depressurized as someone entered the room.

"Good evening," the visitor said.

Teddy turned toward the voice, disappointed to find that someone had beaten him to it again. However, to his surprise, his visitor wasn't a nurse in a blue-suit but an elderly man in a white lab coat. He seemed to be in his late sixties, his face tanned and lined with wrinkles, with the remnants of his silver hair slicked back from a receding hairline. A stethoscope hung around his neck, and a FEMA ID card dangled from his coat's lapel, while his breast pocket overflowed with an assortment of pens and markers.

"I'm Doctor Gatsby," the man said in an affable voice. He walked to Teddy's bedside and extended a hand. "It's nice to meet you, Mr. Sanders."

Teddy hesitated, but then weakly shook the man's hand even though that simple act felt overly laborious. Gatsby offered him a smile, and Teddy saw the unmistakable glint of intelligence in the man's blue eyes, as well as something else that he couldn't quite place a finger on.

The doctor withdrew his hand and turned toward the monitor, carefully scrutinizing the readings. Teddy had a million questions, and it felt like he was going to blurt them all out at the same time in an unintelligible string of words, but one eventually rose above them all.

"When can I leave?"

"You're lucky that they picked you up when they did," the doctor replied, ignoring his question. "The bullet missed your femoral artery, but you almost succumbed to exsanguination."

Teddy stared at him with a vacant expression. The doctor glanced down at him and must have seen his confusion.

"Blood loss, Mr. Sanders," he clarified with a pitying smile. "You nearly bled to death in the middle of the road."

Teddy remembered he wasn't the only one in bad shape. "What about the sergeant?"

"Dead," Gatsby coldly replied as he turned his attention back to the monitor. "He expired two weeks ago."

Teddy was surprised at just how much time had passed since he'd been admitted. "How?"

"Retroperitoneal hemorrhaging caused by a ruptured aortic aneurysm," the doctor explained. "There was very little we could do, given his injuries."

Teddy didn't know what half of that meant, but he understood dead. He knew that the hard-ass lieutenant wouldn't have taken the news well, but he hoped that meant he would rescind the offer he made. Hock didn't seem like the type of man who took refusal very well.

The doctor, seemingly oblivious to Teddy's predicament, continued. "Your initial prognosis wasn't very good; I was concerned about infection. Fortunately, I think you're out of the woods. Everything has healed well, and we've removed the buckshot pellets that were embedded in your thoracic region."

Gatsby lifted Teddy's gown and peeled back the gauze bandage wrapped around his thigh. He peered down at the healing wound, nodded with approval, and carefully reapplied the bandaging. He pulled out a small notepad from his pocket and scribbled something.

Teddy placed a hand over his eyes. The longer he kept them open, the dizzier he became. Whatever drugs they were pumping into him seemed to have lasting effects.

"If everything looks so fucking rosy, then why do they keep forcing medication down my throat?" he asked with his hand still over his eyes.

"For the pain." Gatsby placed a cold hand on Teddy's shoulder and gave him an empty smile. "We don't want you suffering while we work."

Teddy removed his hand and gave the doctor a dark look; he was lying. It didn't take a genius to figure out that the liberal dispensation of heavy sedatives had nothing to do with pain management and everything to do with behavioral compliance. It was a tactic he had seen in Tucson. The prison doctors kept many of the troublemakers in line with their needles. Sometimes, they housed heavily medicated schizophrenic inmates in the general population to avoid having to provide proper medical treatment for their illness. Whenever someone started making too much trouble, a shot of chlorpromazine always seemed to do the trick.

"Doc, what the fuck is going on?" Teddy asked weakly. "And what's the deal with the space suits?"

Gatsby flashed a slight smile and put his notepad away. "Do you know much about immunology, Mr. Sanders?" Teddy simply looked at him, annoyed, until the doctor chuckled. "I gather not. But, if you did, you'd understand my fascination with you."

A dark thought crossed Teddy's mind. "Doc, spare me the bullshit and tell me."

"Tell you what?"

"Am I sick? Do I have the flu again?"

"Quite the contrary—you're immune!"

Teddy grew even more confused. "I can't be totally immune. I had the flu once."

"Exactly," the doctor replied. "You weren't immune, but now you are. You had the flu, recovered, and developed an immunity to that strain."

"Many others had it and got better, too. I don't understand why I'm so special."

"Your body's immune response makes you unique," the doctor explained. "Most people develop antibodies to a particular strain and then become susceptible as their immune response to the initial infection naturally declines. The blood sample they took at the quarantine center back in Tucson revealed H7N9 antibodies, but that's expected in a recovered individual. If I were to compare the numbers from that initial test to the numbers I've taken in this clinic after you lost so much blood, I would expect to see a drastic reduction in your immune response to the H7N9 pathogen. However, yours is still going strong; the presence of abundant antibodies in your blood is testament to that."

"Then why the space suits?"

"Even more fascinating is the way your system responds to antigenic drift," the doctor went on as if he didn't hear the question. He waved his hands animatedly, as if that would make the conversation any easier for Teddy to follow. "Small genetic changes are common with influenza. This genetic drifting creates a new variant of the virus, which doesn't pose a real danger to an immune individual since they're close enough together on the phylogenetic tree that they share the same antigenic properties. A healthy immune system exposed to a similar virus will usually recognize it and respond accordingly. However, small genetic changes can accumulate over time and result in viruses that differ vastly from the original. When that happens, the body's immune system cannot recognize it, and a second wave of infection occurs."

"I still don't understand why that means anything to me," Teddy grumbled.

"Because your body is different!" the doctor exclaimed. "This strain of avian influenza drifts more than any other I've studied at length. Its instability makes it difficult to even create a baseline vaccine; as soon as we manufacture one, the virus changes. What astounds me is the way your body can take the antigenic drifts in stride! Not only do you not get sick, but your body produces antibodies for every variant you're introduced to."

"That doesn't make sense." Teddy shook his head out of sheer aggravation. "I haven't been exposed to any new strains of the flu. The only sick people I've been around were back at the stadium."

Gatsby cleared his throat and adjusted his glasses. "That's not entirely true. You see, as soon as I recognized your body's abnormally robust response, I had to test a theory. We've injected you with several mutated forms of the virus during your stay here." He chuckled at his own ingenuity. "One nasty concoction had every variant we've discovered so far, and I was sure that even you would succumb to it. But, you didn't!"

Suddenly, the reason for those space suits became horrifyingly clear.

"You…infected me?" Teddy asked incredulously.

"No, we didn't infect you," the doctor said as he took a step back and visibly measured his words. "We exposed you. Your blood will give us the best chance yet to create a viable vaccine. In fact, if we can get your antibodies to replicate in laboratory animals, then we can even begin passive immunization therapy."

"You could've killed me!" Teddy floundered weakly on the bed to get up, but his body wouldn't respond. "You sadistic motherfucker!"

Gatsby took a step back, visibly shaken by his display of rage, but adopted a somewhat calmer tone as he said, "Please be rational. While I am positive there are others out there like you, the odds of us discovering someone in this camp are highly unlikely. Your help will benefit countless lives."

"I've lost every life that matters to me!" Teddy snarled. "I couldn't care less about the rest of the goddamn world. I'm not helping you!"

Gatsby blinked and then calmly adjusted his glasses with a smile. "You don't really have a choice in the matter anymore."

He waved a hand at one of the cameras mounted on the ceiling. The door opened, and three blue-suits entered. One of them held an MP5 submachine gun.

"Take him off of the monitors and wheel him down to phlebotomy," Gatsby ordered.

Two of the blue-suits went to work disconnecting the electrodes from Teddy's body and turning off the monitoring equipment, while the blue-suit holding the MP5 stood at the foot of the bed with his weapon pointed at Teddy.

"I want out of here!" Teddy demanded. "No more tests! No more of this bullshit!"

"You'll get your wish as soon as I get enough blood," Gatsby assured. "I'll send you off with that madman lieutenant, and this will all be nothing more than a bad memory."

One of the blue-suits disconnected the IV from his arm.

"No! No blood!"

"Don't be childish," the doctor chided with another pitying smile. "You'll be fine. I don't need much. And if I need more, I can always have you brought to me."

"I don't give you permission!" Teddy exclaimed.

The statement brought chuckles from everyone in the room. Teddy stilled, his body exhausted from struggling against his chemical restraints. He stared up at the ceiling and drew in rapid, shallow breaths. The blue-suits rolled his hospital bed into a brightly lit hallway. Gatsby and the blue-suit with the MP5 followed.

Teddy looked around, squinting at the light. Pipes and ductwork were suspended along the ceiling and interspersed with harsh white light fixtures. He noticed that many other rooms in that section of the hall had doors just like his. Each was spray-painted with a number. Teddy wasn't sure how many rooms had people locked away inside, but he knew that this meant he wasn't their only test subject.

At the end of the hall, they passed a glassed-in security booth manned by an officer who had her feet up on the desk and her nose in a book. The blue-suits rolled the bed around the corner and took him down an adjacent hall. Long observation windows lined both sides of the hall, along with two pressurized steel doors. A red sign on each of the doors read, BSL-4 PPE required beyond this point!

On the other side of the glass, Teddy saw men, women, and children inside a plain, dormitory-style room. Each of them had a tattoo on the back of their left hand: a square-shaped pattern of dots. Their beds, which consisted of little more than bare-bones cots, were arranged in six rows, and each had a tiny footlocker. The patients wore white hospital gowns and stared at him with intrigue as he rolled past them.

Gatsby followed Teddy's gaze and motioned for the blue-suits to stop in the middle of the hall.

"What's on their hands?"

"What do you mean?" the doctor asked.

"What do you think I mean?" Teddy pointed at the back of his own left hand. "What do those dots mean?"

"Inventory…" Teddy's stomach churned. "You're a fucking Nazi."

Gatsby seemed taken aback by his outburst. "You don't understand. It is imperative that we can readily identity and track these individuals."

"Why?" Teddy asked.

"Because they are what we're up against," the doctor said as he approached the glass and waved a hand at the people inside. "They are the biggest danger we face."

"A bunch of innocent people?" He stared at them again, looking for some sign of a threat. They looked frightened, tired, and uneasy, but not sinister. "They don't even look sick."

"No, they don't, and they never will," the doctor said. "At face value, they appear completely healthy, but they're all very sick and therefore very dangerous. You see, the quarantine centers are laughable. The people who take the blood samples and decide based on those results are inexperienced doctors, unqualified technicians, or even soldiers. Once they see antibodies and no manifestation of symptoms, they mark the person as healthy. They're so eager to ship out healthy bodies to the camps."

"You're talking in circles," Teddy huffed. "I thought you said antibodies were a good thing."

"The presence of antibodies in the blood is one thing, but the presence of the H7N9 pathogen is another," Gatsby said with a condescending smile. "I double-check the camp's results and quarantine the patients who have abnormalities. I am the only reason our camp is going strong, because I only allow trains to come in from quarantine centers who take the time to draw blood—such as yours did."

"Quarantine them for what?" The pompous asshole was getting on Teddy's nerves, and it took most of his quickly draining self-control to stop himself from punching the good doctor in the nose.

"I suspect that they're all asymptomatic carriers of the virus," Gatsby explained. "They can transmit the disease, but not at the same rate as symptomatic individuals, which creates an invisible reservoir for the virus. Inside them, the virus continues to drift and change. Just one asymptomatic carrier is enough to take down an entire camp, as we have seen time and time again since this pandemic started."

Teddy realized he could have been stuck in that room if that doctor prick deemed something in his blood unfavorable. "Who are you to second-guess other doctors?"

"I've been in the field of infectious disease for over twenty years."

"That doesn't mean shit to me. You just want some people to experiment on," Teddy accused. "They're not infectious. You're a goddamn liar."

"No, but sometimes the truth isn't pleasant," the doctor said calmly. "Asymptomatic carriers are the reason most of the quarantine centers are failing. You can't isolate people purely based on symptoms with the existence of these carriers. Many quarantine centers forgo blood tests and rely on rapid field tests based on the original H7N9 pathogen, but those are becoming antiquated because of the emergence of new strains."

"Your fear tactics won't work on me," Teddy snarled. "I think you're full of shit."

The doctor stared at him. "I'm not trying to frighten you. I'm trying to illustrate just how badly we need someone like you. I thought that if you knew what we were up against, then maybe you'd be more willing to work with us rather than view us as some sort of adversary."

"Go to hell," Teddy sneered. "I couldn't care less if your whole miserable system fell apart."

Gatsby sighed and motioned for the blue-suits to resume the trip down the hall.

"I suppose it doesn't matter," the doctor said as he followed behind. "I need your blood, not your understanding. A compliant patient makes for an easier procedure."

Teddy kept quiet—he didn't feel like arguing with the man anymore. Instead, he stared at the faces behind the glass as the blue-suits rolled him down the hall. Seated on one cot, he spotted a man—no, a boy. He sat alone with his face in his hands. His purple hair was reverting to its original shade of brown at the roots, and his skin was a dull, pasty shade. Just like the others, his left hand bore a tattooed datamatrix code.

Teddy's heart stopped when recognition struck him.

"Ein!" he exclaimed, briefly breaking through his mental haze.

Ein lowered his hands and looked up with tired eyes. His expression lit up as soon as he saw Teddy.

Then, his bed was pushed past the window, and there was a concrete wall between them.

"No! Stop!" Teddy pleaded as he tried to force his numb body to sit up. "Get him out of there!"

"Who?" the doctor asked.

"The kid with the purple hair!" Teddy shouted. "He's not sick! Get him out of that room!"

Teddy lifted his head and shoulders up off of the bed about five inches, but was quickly pinned down again as one of the blue-suits pressed their hand against his chest.

"Stay down!" the blue-suit ordered, his voice barely decipherable through his respirator.

"Restrain him," the doctor said. "If he refuses to comply, we will treat him accordingly."

The blue-suits stopped pushing and secured Teddy's wrists and ankles to the bed with ambulatory restraints. The man holding the MP5 once again pointed his weapon at him in a less than subtle threat.

"Get him out of there!" Teddy yelled again as he struggled weakly against the restraints. "He's not sick!"

The blue-suits finished restraining him and stepped back as they wheezed through their respirators. Teddy stopped resisting; he had no more strength, and his demands had fallen on deaf ears.

They continued on once again. Teddy's head lolled from side to side as he stared up at the ceiling.

At least I know where he is. I'll get you out of there, kid—somehow.

They wheeled him down another corridor, through a set of double doors, and into a partitioned room overlooked by a glassed-in nursing station. The blue-suits rolled Teddy into one of the open sections and walked away. The armed blue-suit stayed behind and stood next to the doctor.

Gatsby motioned at the nursing station without looking. "I need fifteen milliliters."

Two male nurses wearing scrubs emerged and carefully inserted a needle into the port that was still taped to Teddy's forearm.

"Make a fist," one nurse ordered.

Teddy ignored the nurse and glared at the doctor. The nurse jabbed until he found a vein, but Teddy didn't flinch.

"You're a goddamn vampire," Teddy snarled.

The doctor raised his brows and adjusted his glasses. "Give him the propofol infusion. I don't need his impertinent attitude."

The nurse nodded and retrieved a syringe from the station.

"You'll get more than my attitude if I ever get the chance," Teddy warned.

"Doubtful," Gatsby said with little concern. "In case you haven't figured it out yet, your survival depends on your usefulness to me. That lieutenant is irrelevant. My work holds more value than his fiefdom."

After they finished drawing two vials of blood, they injected Teddy with propofol. He fell silent as a wave of lightheadedness struck him and his ears rang. Several seconds passed, and Teddy's symptoms worsened. His vision became blurry, so he closed his eyes.

They didn't open again.

15

When Teddy next awoke, he found himself in yet another unfamiliar room. It had bare, white walls and two rows of plastic chairs that were bolted to the floor. A clock hung on the wall, and the second hand ticked away dutifully.

Teddy was thankful for the clock, because it finally gave him some semblance of time: eleven past seven. Morning or evening, he couldn't be sure, but at least he had some sort of reference point.

It reminded him of a waiting room. Thanks to the clock, he knew he had been waiting for over three hours. Teddy did not know who or what he was waiting for, but he felt confident that it would involve the one person he dreaded seeing the most.

After all, the lieutenant said they'd talk again, and he seemed like the kind of man who kept his word.

He had been moved out of his hospital bed and placed in a wheelchair. The ambulatory restraints were gone, but that didn't matter, since he was still recovering from the medication they had flooded his system with. Even as the propofol cocktail wore off, Teddy's legs felt like jelly, and he was dog-tired.

Under the clock, there was a single door. If he wasn't confident that his body would let him down, he would've already attempted to get out of the chair and make a run for it.

Which was probably the reason they had an armed officer standing next to him with his hand resting on the butt of a holstered pistol. The officer—a skinny, young kid who looked like he had just finished high school—had not said a word to him.

Teddy sluggishly turned his head toward the officer. "Do they give you hazard pay to hold sick folks at gunpoint, or is this just for fun?"

The officer swallowed hard and purposefully kept his eyes fixed on the door ahead. His grip on the pistol tightened as his hand started trembling.

Teddy tsked and turned his attention back to the door. "Pathetic—just like the rest of them."

"Shut up, or I'll have you swinging," the officer said in a muted voice.

"I wasn't aware that they had built a wheelchair ramp for the gallows," Teddy said. The officer scowled and reached a hand up to slap him, but Teddy added, "Careful. Don't you know who wants to see me and how important I am? If you lay a hand on me, Hock won't be too pleased. *You* might be the one swinging."

The officer flushed, lowered his hand, and went back to staring at the door with a wide-eyed, vacant expression. Several more minutes passed in silence, but eventually, a rough voice came through the officer's radio.

"Bring him out."

Teddy felt an odd mixture of relief, fear, and apprehension. While he was happy to get away from the doctor, he knew that nothing good awaited him. Roger died, and Ein remained locked up.

The officer pushed the wheelchair through the door and out into a narrow hallway. Faded signage offering directions to the boiler room, watershed, and the central supply storage room were bolted to the wall. Between that and the exposed pipes and ductwork along the ceiling, whatever the place used to be, it was never intended to be a hospital.

Navigating the maze on his own would prove difficult, so Teddy tried to create a rudimentary mental map for when he returned to get Ein. It was no use; the vanilla walls blended together in his mind.

At the end of the hallway, they arrived at an elevator that had a bunch of mop buckets stacked next to it. The silver doors slid open as soon as they got close. The officer rolled Teddy inside and then pressed his ID badge against a scanner. It was sloppily attached next to the buttons, almost as if it was an afterthought.

The doors slid shut, and the lift ascended. Teddy glanced at his reflection and had to avert his gaze. He looked as if he had aged ten years over the last few months.

When they came to a stop and the doors slid open, Teddy found himself in a lobby reminiscent of an old office building. There was an abandoned reception desk in the center, along with two unmanned metal detectors covered with cobwebs. Darkened office suites branched off on either side of them, and a row of tinted, glass sliding doors took up the entire wall across from the elevator. Half of the overhead lights were on, and dust covered everything after fluttering out of the vents.

Teddy craned his neck and saw that the elevator he came out of was part of a group of four. Theirs appeared to be the only one that functioned. Above them, there was a faded United States Border Patrol emblem with *Midwestern Regional Detention Division* embossed in tarnished brass letters.

A few yards ahead, just past the empty reception desk and in front of the entrance doors, Hock leaned against one of the marble pillars with his arms crossed over his chest. He wore a peacoat dusted with snow and jackboots, but his typically meticulous attention to detail just wasn't there. Grime caked Hock's boots and his lapels noticeably lacked insignias. A military dress cap with a patent leather peak shrouded the upper portion of his face in shadow.

The fact that the lieutenant looked troubled wasn't lost on Teddy.

Behind the lieutenant stood a black man wearing a tan overcoat and jeans. An orange knit skullcap covered his head. The top part of his left arm featured a red band. It took Teddy a few moments to realize that the man was Perry. His gut was gone, and his face was thinner. It looked as if he had dropped at least twenty pounds since Teddy last saw him.

The officer stopped the wheelchair a few feet away from the lieutenant.

"Not much to look at, is it?" Hock's voice echoed off of the walls and reverberated down the empty halls. "This building was part of the original immigration detention camp. I've heard the rumors, but people have overactive imaginations when it comes to things that they know nothing about. Once things settle down, I'm going to convert the old offices upstairs," the lieutenant continued when Teddy kept silent. "I'm moving my men out of those cramped military dorms and into their own suites."

Again, Teddy said nothing.

"That doesn't sound appealing to you?" the lieutenant asked.

"That sounds just fucking peachy…except for the part about the secret lab," Teddy countered.

"It's a basement," Hock casually corrected. "That doctor believes that a few renovations have turned that derelict space into a modern laboratory. Once we're settled in, I'm moving his entire operation to the old dorms."

"I'm sure he'll object."

"I'm sure he will, but I don't take orders from him," Hock said indignantly. He glanced over at Teddy for the first time and seemed alarmed by his appearance. "Christ, son…what did he do to you?"

"You already know what he did to me," Teddy replied flatly.

"I don't."

"Bullshit."

Hock studied him for a moment. "Believe it or not, I'm not as callous as you think. I've made a conscious decision not to get involved in his work. I tolerate him because circumstances force me to—that's all."

"Yet your soldiers and trains bring him the bodies he needs for his sadistic experiments," Teddy said. "There's a difference between tolerance and enabling."

"That's just another compromise forced on me. In order to get my initial troop numbers up, I was forced to agree to work at a camp that took part in the government's ongoing vaccination research program." Hock rubbed the bridge of his nose. "I know. It's a bullshit explanation, but navigating bullshit becomes second nature when you're in the military." Hock sighed and raised the peak of his cap, staring down at Teddy with tired eyes. "When I was deployed in Iraq so many years ago, a group of militants had taken refuge in a small village outside of Kirkuk. I'm not sure how many there were—probably close to one hundred— but they really gave us hell. The brass decided to use a series of GBU-43s to eliminate the threat—"

"What does that have to do with anything?" Teddy interjected.

"It was a bullshit compromise," he answered. "In order to kill one hundred militants, close to two thousand innocent villagers had to be collateral damage. An acceptable loss."

"That's horrible," Teddy said, at a loss for words. The callous approach taken by the military towards the pandemic probably made sense to them. The ends justified the means, after all.

"But it's also the truth," the lieutenant admitted. "The mission always trumps common decency, and most of the time it even trumps common sense. The lack of foresight is the reason we're having the trouble we're experiencing right now. They're too focused on their medical mission and not focused enough on law and order."

"What trouble?" Teddy asked.

"Patience is wearing thin."

"Why? What happened?"

"Exactly what I thought would happen," the lieutenant shot back. "I took it hard when I lost Parham. He was a good soldier who handled the bullshit with ease. Ever since, I've had to hire cowards, thieves, and half-wits who're unworthy of wearing a uniform."

The lieutenant gave the officer beside Teddy an icy glare; the officer shifted his weight uncomfortably and looked down at the floor.

"I know you'll be different—I see the same potential in you as I did in Parham." Hock's expression hardened. "So, what will it be? Will you join me or not?"

Teddy's first impulse was the same as it was the day the lieutenant initially made him the offer—if it could be called as much. Not only did he want to blatantly refuse, but he also wanted to inform the man exactly which orifice he could shove the offer in question.

However, after seeing Ein, his stance wavered.

He'd never be able to storm the castle, guns blazing, and just walk out with Ein unscathed. At best, he'd get killed. At worst, he'd get Ein killed along with him. If he had a uniform, at least he'd be able to come and go without raising too many eyebrows. As much as he hated to admit it, the lieutenant's offer might be the only way out.

Teddy couldn't speak aloud—his tongue was too sharp and his emotions were too raw—but he nodded.

"Glad to have you." Hock glanced down at the wheelchair. "You can still walk, right?"

"Once the drugs wear off," he answered in a more caustic tone than he intended.

Hock didn't appear bothered by it and just nodded. "Given your current state, you won't be much use to me right now. Rest and get your strength back, then we'll talk."

Teddy frowned. How could he rest when he knew Ein was stuck in that hamster cage? "If it's all the same to you, I'd like to get started sooner rather than later."

Hock seemed pleased. He rubbed a finger against his chin as he considered their options. "Do you think you'll be okay after a good night's rest?"

"I do."

Hock smiled and waved Perry over. "Help Sanders get changed into something suitable and take him back to the dorm. I'll send someone to retrieve him in the morning."

"Yes, sir," Perry said tiredly.

Teddy stared up at him and noticed just how malnourished he seemed.

Perry pulled his cracked lips into a forced smile and extended his hand. "Can you stand?"

Teddy took the bony hand and pulled himself up off the chair. It felt like every nerve in his leg protested as a wave of sharp, stabbing pain radiated up his legs and into his chest, but miraculously, he was able to remain on his feet. His knees buckled, but Perry grasped his wrist and drew his arm around his neck to help support him.

"I hope I got your size right. I picked out something a little warmer than I did when you first got here," Perry said. "Weather took quite a turn since I last saw you."

As he was led across the lobby toward one of the empty offices, Teddy couldn't help but wonder what else had changed.

16

A sharp wind blew snow off the dormitory overhangs. Dark, dense clouds shrouded the setting sun, promising even more icy precipitation throughout the night.

Helping to support his weight, Perry led Teddy along a slick footpath between the dorms. Teddy wore two sweatshirts, layered pants, and a thick jacket, but the frigid air still pricked at any exposed skin and made him shiver. Indeed, the weather had changed, but the other changes that had occurred since he last walked around the camp were much more striking in comparison.

The tent cities, vendor stalls, and clotheslines that were once erected in the alleyways and that used to spill out into the footpaths had been abandoned and were now lost to snowbanks. All the steel drums that were once used for firepits were either toppled or filled with debris. Graffiti covered most of the walls and some of the dorm's doors; slogans like DEATH TO FACISTS and NO FOOD, NO WORK had become commonplace.

The most haunting change for Teddy was the lack of people. Even though the sun hadn't sunk yet, the pathways and alleys were entirely devoid of civilians. The community that once consisted of laughing children and folks swapping the day's gossip had been replaced by jackbooted officers. Even the mangy mutts and stray cats were gone.

Teddy bleakly wondered for a moment if everyone was dead. As if to support his dark thoughts, his eyes happened on the frozen, skeletal remains of a dog half buried in a mound of snow. He thought of Roger's dog, Zoey—of the goofy smile that had seemed to be permanently fixed on her furry face—and glanced away from the corpse.

"Where is everyone?" he asked.

As if on cue, a recorded announcement played over the camp's PA system. "Attention: due to terrorist activity, curfew is in full effect. Any resident caught outside will be subject to arrest."

"That doesn't apply to us orderlies or you, since this brief trip is authorized," Perry assured. "I'm your escort, so you'll be fine."

"What terrorist activity?"

Two officers hurried past them, their rifles held at the ready, and quickly turned the next corner.

Perry remained tight-lipped until the officers were well out of earshot. "I'm not sure. While I was waiting for you with the lieutenant, I heard that there was some sort of fuss near dorm eight."

"How?"

"They were blabbering over the radio before the lieutenant figured I was probably listening and turned the volume down," Perry explained. "I don't know the details. We'll see soon enough since we have to pass that dorm."

"How long has this been going on?"

"Ever since they got stricter with the rationing." Perry frowned and shook his head. "It's a shame how folks have been acting. They're frustrated and taking it out on the uniforms—even in our own homes. Bunch of damn fools, if you ask me."

Teddy remembered the incident at the dining hall the morning that the new rationing was announced. He wasn't surprised that the violence had escalated. "It was a long time coming if they still ain't feeding folks properly."

"It's uncalled for and barbaric," Perry argued. "If people would calm down and do what they're told, we wouldn't have so many problems."

Teddy rolled his eyes. "It sounds like you're the same pacifist I remember."

"Old Perry is a survivor…I never bite the hand that feeds me."

The word coward seemed more fitting, but Teddy didn't argue the point.

"If they fed folks, most of their trouble might go away," he said instead.

"It'll pass," his escort curtly replied.

"What about the work crews?"

"They stopped those a while ago. Security concerns."

They rounded the corner, following the same path the officers had taken moments earlier. He knew this route well; it led from the dorms toward the dining hall, passing the ominous gallows. The walk was laborious and slow, the biting cold seeming to stiffen his joints and further hinder his already unsteady gait. More officers jogged past them, a blur of urgency in the chilling air.

As they neared the gallows, the recording repeated across the camp's speakers. "Attention: due to terrorist activity, curfew is in full effect. Any resident caught outside will be subject to arrest."

When they passed by the gallows, Teddy found himself once again surprised. The scaffolding support pillars had been hacked apart, and the platform had caved in. The gibbets on top leaned in every direction, and the empty nooses swung lazily in the freezing air.

As Perry followed Teddy's gaze, his face contorted with disgust. His brow furrowed and his lips curled into a tight grimace. "Goddamn animals…no respect for the law. A mob did that a week ago. They had us on lockdown for two whole days because of that little stunt," he said, his voice thick with revulsion as he spat out the words.

"Are they any worse than the animals who strung folks up in the first place?" Teddy asked.

Perry's features softened slightly from their previous tension as he moderated his tone. He sighed, shook his head, and continued with a measured calmness. "Thanks to their actions, the authorities have been taking harsher measures against offenders."

"What sort of measures?"

"Before your accident, did you meet anyone from dorm thirty— where the woodworkers were housed?" Perry asked.

"No clue."

"Well, you won't anymore. They executed the whole dorm for that stunt."

Teddy, visibly shaken, looked at him, his mouth agape and the cold momentarily forgotten. "An entire dorm? You're bluffing."

"Wish I were. Men, women, and children all paid the price because a few idiots acted up."

"Those tactics are going to come back and bite them in the tail," Teddy said with a sneer. "Folks won't stand for it."

Perry shook his head. "After they took out that dorm, things quieted down for a while. It started getting bad again just a few days ago. They're going to force the authorities' hands *again*. Wait and see!"

Teddy found the man's apologist attitude toward their captures disgusting, yet he knew better than to argue against the very people he was about to be employed by if he wanted to maintain a believable cover long enough to save Ein.

Two hundred yards past the ruined gallows, they came across a line of officers holding riot shields and cordoning off an alleyway between dormitories eight and nine. Fresh blood peppered the snow at their feet. Perry and Teddy slowed their progress as they craned their necks to peer down the alley. Sickly horror turned Teddy's stomach as one of the guard tower's searchlights revealed the gruesome scene.

Four officers, their faces battered beyond recognition, hung from the dormitory roof. Orange extension cords cut into their swollen necks and created a web of ruptured purple veins just under their skin. Their uniforms had been stripped of weapons, and a message was spray-painted on the wall over their heads.

You take ours; we take yours—oink, oink.

Another group of officers was on the roof, hacking away at one of the cords with a dull pocketknife. After a few moments, the cord snapped, and the body struck the ground with a thud.

Perry recoiled, but Teddy couldn't look away from the dangling corpses as fear squeezed his heart. Was that the fate that awaited him when he donned the uniform? Would his attackers even give him enough time to explain himself? Would they even care?

"Keep it moving!" an officer holding a riot shield growled.

Perry nudged Teddy forward, his hooded eyes focused on the ground. "Fucking animals…"

Teddy staggered along in a daze as the ramifications of his deal with the lieutenant hit home.

They stopped again when officers kicked in the doors to dormitories eight, nine, and seven. They grabbed men and women seemingly at random and pulled them out into the snow by their hair as they screamed and protested. Gunfire erupted from inside two of the dorms, and Teddy flinched at each individual shot.

The pleasant, even-keeled voice of the recorded announcer played throughout the camp and cut through the cacophony. "Attention: due to terrorist activity, curfew is in full effect. Any resident caught outside will be subject to arrest."

"Let's keep moving," Perry insisted. "We don't want to get caught in the middle of this."

Teddy tried to shuffle faster, but the adrenaline in his veins couldn't overpower his injuries or the effects of the drugs the doctor had loaded him up on. Their dorm was only a few more buildings away, but the distance seemed to grow with each crack of gunfire.

Both men came to an abrupt stop as dormitory fifteen's door flung open and five officers armed with rifles forced a group of men and women outside. Terrified children watched from the doorway and cried out for their parents, but were kept inside by a single officer wielding a truncheon.

"On your knees!" the officer screamed.

The group of terrified civilians did as they were told, but a few who were not fast enough or showed a hint of resistance were struck in the face with the butt of a rifle.

"Hands on your head!" another officer shouted as he brandished his weapon at the group.

The civilians who were still conscious complied.

An officer spun toward Perry and Teddy and pointed his rifle at them. "On the ground! Hands on your heads!"

"I'm an orderly!" Perry shouted back. "Lieutenant Hock asked me to bring this man back to dorm twenty!"

The officer shone his weapon's tactical light on Perry's armband and seemed to relax a little. He stepped aside and waved them by. "Then get to your dorm!"

Perry rushed Teddy through the wretched crowd and past the row of uniforms. Teddy squeezed his eyes shut; he knew what was coming.

The crying intensified, and then a series of deafening gunshots forever silenced it.

Teddy dared not turn around to witness the carnage. He let himself be blindly led to the dorm, rage boiling inside him. It took every ounce of his resolve not to lash out fruitlessly at the executioners like a rabid, wounded animal.

Perry came to a stop. "We're here…we made it."

Teddy opened his teary eyes and watched as Perry placed his forearm against the door's scanner. A robotic female voice greeted him as the door unlocked.

Perry brought Teddy inside, slammed the door shut behind them, and smiled as if the massacre that had just happened had all been a bad dream. "You still have your old bed."

Teddy glared daggers at the man. He felt like ripping that collaborator's throat out with his bare hands. Instead, he tore away from his supporting arm and limped across the room to his bunk.

Perry called out to his back, "Things will get better."

Teddy bit his tongue and looked around, immediately noticing that most of the bunks were empty. That tracked; most of the crew died on that highway. He plopped down on his cot, leaned over to brace his elbows on his knees, and cradled his face in his frostbitten hands.

A whimper interrupted his troubled thoughts. Teddy lowered his hands and looked toward the noise to find Zoey. She was much thinner and missing patches of her coat, and she approached him cautiously, her ears lowered. Her tail gave a few cautious wags, but she kept her distance.

"Zoey," Teddy said, as his gloomy expression brightened. "Is that you, girl?"

Her tail wagged a little more enthusiastically, and she gave an eager yip. Within seconds, she had her paws on his chest and was licking his face. Teddy laughed and made a half-hearted attempt to convince her to get down, even though he relished every moment. Zoey's tail swung back and forth with such intensity that she could barely balance on her hind legs.

"Easy, girl!" Teddy said after he got his laughter under control. He smiled and scratched behind her ears. "I sure as hell missed you, too. I can't believe you remember me!"

Zoey responded with a few overjoyed barks.

Perry walked over with his hands in his pockets. "I brought her in after the accident. It seemed a shame to just let her die out there, especially when the snow started falling. She was Roger's dog, right?"

"Yeah, she was," Teddy answered, genuinely surprised that Perry of all people cared enough to make such a gesture.

Perry smiled. "I've been feeding her old canned scraps that I had stashed away. I think she's happy to have some company, though. It's awfully quiet in here these days, in case you can't tell."

"Yeah," Teddy said. "It's empty."

"Empty," Perry agreed. He glanced around and then turned his attention back to Teddy. "Anyway, rest up. I guess they'll come get you tomorrow."

He turned and walked away.

"Perry," Teddy called out and waited until the other man had stopped and looked over his shoulder. "Thanks for saving her."

Perry nodded and kept walking.

Teddy flopped back on his cot, and Zoey hopped up and stretched out next to him as her tail continued to wag. He stared up at the empty bunk above him and absently stroked her matted fur. Gunshots came and went, and he slowly lost the good-humored smile the reappearance of a loyal friend had inspired. He was tired and weak, but he knew he wouldn't be able to get any truly restful sleep that night.

17

Teddy walked out of the shower with a towel draped around his neck. Even though he was given a fresh set of clothes, he still felt filthy. No amount of showering would rid himself of the grime he felt festering inside.

Perry sat on the edge of his bunk and watched with amusement as Zoey went at an old can of sardines as if it were a gourmet meal. He turned his head as Teddy approached.

"Feeling better, or do you still have weak knees?"

"All that's gone as far as I can tell. I'm still a little dizzy, but that's probably from hunger more than anything." Teddy stared down at Zoey's food and felt his stomach rumble. "You don't have any more of those, do you?"

Perry gave him a puzzled look and then laughed. "Sure, but they're all dented or expired. You'd get a case of botulism."

Teddy groaned and put a hand on his stomach. "At this point, it's almost worth the risk."

Perry laughed again. Zoey looked up from her food, licked her lips, and barked at Teddy. Her tail started swinging excitedly. Teddy crouched down and smiled as the dog bounded over and licked at his face.

"Easy, girl!" Teddy laughed. "You'll have me stinking like fish, and I just took a shower!"

Zoey gave a few more joyous barks and a couple of sloppy licks and then trotted back to her food.

Teddy got to his feet and wiped her slobber off his cheeks with the towel. "Is the curfew over?"

"I think so since the door is unlocked, but I haven't been out to see how things look." Perry frowned. "It sounded bad last night. Did you hear the gunshots?"

"Yeah…couldn't sleep."

"I guess they feel they've made their point, but I don't agree with the overzealous way they handled it."

"That's funny, because last night I remember you calling the regular folks a bunch of animals," he said humorlessly.

Perry shook his head. "Both sides share blame. People need to learn how to get along."

"It sounds like people would do that if they just had some decent food in their bellies."

"What if there is no more food to give?" Perry countered.

Teddy considered that for a moment and then shook his head. "They always have emergency supplies…contingency plans and shit."

"I don't think they do this time."

"Christ, Perry, I thought you were the eternal optimist. We can't both be cynical pricks."

Perry chuckled. "Maybe you're right, but it gets hard sometimes. Everybody knows I'm all alone, and they don't take too kindly to us red bands. I get nervous walking outside on my own these days."

"Fuck other people—you have Zoey," Teddy offered.

"That I do," Perry said with a smile.

There was an urgent knock on the door just before the electronic lock disengaged, as if it'd been overridden. As the door opened, a gust of wind sent flakes of fresh snow across the floor. Zoey tucked her tail between her legs and ran off to hide under one of the empty bunks as two officers wearing woolen peacoats and balaclavas entered the room. The visors of their riot helmets hooded their eyes as they scanned the room with their tactical lights and then focused their beams on Teddy.

"Teddy Sanders?" one of them asked.

"Yeah?"

The officers turned off their lights and lowered their weapons. "Come with us."

"Take care of yourself out there," Perry said.

Teddy followed the officers outside and looked over his shoulder at Perry. "You, too, old man."

As Teddy walked alongside the officers down the footpath, he noticed signs of the previous night's chaos subtly obscured by nearly six inches of fresh snow. Splotches of blood were sealed beneath thick ice, where spent brass casings glinted gold and orange in the morning sun.

Dormitories, their doors ripped off just hours earlier, now stood muted behind fresh plywood. Signs stapled to the wood declared a quarantine because of typhoid. Even the graffiti that had screamed in anger and defiance was now muted, hastily covered with swathes of white paint.

Despite all of that effort, Teddy knew others must have heard the gunshots. It was clear in how the civilians glowered scornfully at the officers as they passed. Teddy felt choking tension surround him, and he was positive that the officers felt it, too, if the way their eyes darted side to side at every alleyway and every corner was anything to go by.

A pleasant voice announced over the camp's speakers, "Security reminder: due to a rise in confirmed typhoid cases, public gatherings are no longer permitted. Unauthorized groups will be subject to disciplinary action."

As they passed by, Teddy glanced down the alley where they had strung up the officers. The bodies and the extension cords were long gone; even the graffiti had been painted over.

One officer saw Teddy checking out the area. "It's disgusting what happened."

Teddy thought about how the cops slaughtered more than what he assumed were one hundred innocent people in response. "It was."

"Those fucking roaches will think twice before pulling some shit like that again," the officer continued.

The other one, a skinny man with a white skull painted on the back of his riot helmet, shot him a sharp look and jabbed him with his elbow.

"Relax, Hayes. He's one of us now," the first officer said. "He hates them as much as we do."

Hayes looked over his shoulder at Teddy and narrowed his eyes. "I doubt it, Wright. He doesn't look like one of us."

Wright shrugged. "He was handpicked by Hock himself."

"His endorsement doesn't mean much to me," Hayes said as he turned back around. "I haven't been impressed with his decisions lately."

"Yeah, well, that makes two of us, but this is the guy that fucked up all those men that attacked Parham's crew."

"Oh, shit!" Hayes exclaimed. "I didn't know this was the dude…" He studied Teddy with newfound admiration. "That was some good shooting, brother."

"Not really." Teddy maintained eye contact with him. "When you're using a machine gun against a bunch of rednecks, you have the upper hand."

"How many did you lay down?" Hayes asked excitedly.

"I wasn't keeping count. I was just trying to stay alive."

"That's something worth remembering—one hell of a story to share around the fire!"

"How many did you lay down?" Teddy asked.

"What?"

"How many did you guys lay down?" Teddy pointed at one of the plywood-covered dorms.

"Shit…" Hayes thought for a moment. "My crew got at least two hundred."

"Ours had eighty," Wright added.

Teddy's stomach soured. "I didn't know they could fit that many fish in a barrel."

Both Hayes and Wright chuckled, missing the sarcasm in his voice.

"Yeah," Hayes said, a smirk forming on his lips. "Those fucking roaches didn't have much fight in them when we started knocking them down. It took two goddamn hours just to haul their bodies to the pit."

"Did Hock order that?" Teddy asked, masking his disgust with a tone of genuine curiosity.

"He ordered the cleanup," Wright replied, his voice tinged with disdain.

"And the mess itself?" Teddy pressed, playing into their narrative.

Wright shook his head with a smirk. "Didn't have the balls," he said, his voice dripping with contempt. "He's too soft. After they lynched our people like that, we took matters into our own hands."

Hayes pulled down his balaclava and spat on the snow. "They drew first blood."

"Roaches…" Teddy muttered, the word tasting bitter on his tongue, but he let none of that show. "I didn't know that's what you called civilians."

"It's a fitting term," Hayes said, his voice cold, while Wright nodded in agreement.

"Does it apply to everyone?" Teddy asked, his tone neutral, probing.

"What do you mean?" Hayes responded, his brow furrowing slightly.

Teddy kept his expression neutral, hiding his revulsion. "The term. Roaches. Women? Children?" Hayes and Wright glanced at each other, then back at Teddy. There was a pause before Teddy continued, his voice steady. "I'm just trying to understand the rules. After all, it's a mess out there, isn't it?"

"Yeah, it's the same for all of them," Hayes finally responded.

"Roaches…" Teddy echoed softly, as if pondering the term, not letting his anger seep through. He nodded slowly, feigning agreement. "Tough choices in tough times, huh? Seems like you did what you had to do to me."

Wright looked over at Hayes. "I told you. He's one of us."

A voice over the officers' radios broke the silence. "Jayhawk Control to Foxtrot, ten-twenty-five to the central courtyard immediately—ten-forty-four in progress."

"A demonstration?" Hayes asked in disbelief.

Wright shook his head. "I guess they didn't learn. The riot squad is going to whoop their asses."

"Let's hurry and get this rookie over to onboarding so we can get in on the action," Hayes said.

Wright motioned for Teddy to hurry. "Get your gear, and you may get to see some action today."

Teddy continued down the pathway with the two officers on his heels. Out of his peripheral vision, he noticed their weapons were half-cocked and felt more like a prisoner again, but given the conversation they'd just had, that suited him just fine. As he walked, he noticed how empty the paths were. There wasn't a single civilian in sight. A few officers carrying batons and riot shields jogged by, but none of them paid Teddy or his escorts any mind.

"Public gatherings are no longer permitted. Unauthorized groups will be subject to disciplinary action," a voice over the PA reminded them.

As Teddy neared the concrete courtyard where the gallows had once stood, he stopped and stared in awe.

More than a hundred people stood motionless in the middle of the courtyard, their unwavering gaze fixed on the control tower in the middle of the camp. Their numbers seemed to grow as more of them materialized from alleyways and adjacent footpaths. Responding officers lined the edge of the courtyard cautiously and raised their riot shields. Mayville and a small group of officers climbed atop the ruined gallows' scaffolding and pointed their rifles at the crowd.

Mayville brought a megaphone to his mouth and shouted in a high, nasally voice, "Go back to your dorms immediately!"

The crowd didn't move, and, given some of the larger incidents he had witnessed back in the penitentiary, Teddy knew things wouldn't go so easily for Mayville this time around.

Wright prodded Teddy in the back. "Hurry up, grab your gear, and let's break this shit up."

Teddy obeyed, his mind churning. As he picked up his pace and followed Wright, he thought to himself that the brewing chaos might just provide the distraction he needed. They turned the corner and headed down another narrow, empty pathway that ran between two rows of dormitories. It was all very quiet—unnaturally quiet. The officers got jumpier as they passed each alleyway. Their eyes searched wildly for any movement, and they kept checking over their shoulders. Teddy's mind raced as he walked faster, his senses heightened by the growing tension around him.

I just need to get a uniform, a weapon, and an access card, then pick up Ein and get us the fuck out of here.

If everything went smoothly, he could drive straight out of the front gate with a shit-eating grin on his face in no time.

Hayes and Wright kept their weapons at the ready, scanning the dimly lit alleys flanking them. The coppery stench of blood mingled with the sickly sweet aroma of decay seeping out from the open dorm. Teddy thought he glimpsed a shadow moving inside, a hint of an ambush. He kept quiet about it, not wanting to alert Hayes and Wright just yet.

"You brought this shit on yourselves," Teddy finally said, his voice low but firm.

"What are you going on about?" Hayes snapped, turning toward him with a frown. "What did we bring on?"

"Can't you see this place is a ticking bomb?" Teddy responded, his voice rising slightly with urgency. "Between the work details, food rationing, and the squalid conditions—you think people won't snap? Your petty act of revenge last night? That was just the lit match."

"Shut up," Hayes hissed.

"I told you something was off with him," Wright said, suspicion lacing his voice as he pointed his weapon at Teddy. "He's not one of us."

Teddy held his ground, his eyes darting to the shadows moving within the dorm. "I think you're about to have bigger problems to deal with than me."

"What's he going on about?" Hayes demanded, lowering his weapon slightly to glance around, his previous anger now tinged with uncertainty.

Suddenly, a shadow flickered across the rooftop of a nearby dorm.

"Movement!" Wright shouted, pointing upward. "Rooftop—two o'clock!"

They stopped dead in their tracks, rifles aimed skyward, but the figure had already disappeared.

Hayes scanned from one rooftop to another, his face tense. "I don't like this."

"Forget Hock's rules of engagement," Wright muttered, gripping his rifle tighter. "If I see another roach, I'm dropping them."

While their attention was fixed on the rooftops, Teddy noticed a gaunt figure slipping out from an alley, pistol in hand. Wright turned just as the man fired. The shots rang out—three missed, but the last found its mark.

Blood sprayed from Wright's neck as he dropped his rifle and clutched at the wound, staggering. His knees buckled, and he collapsed into the snow, choking on his own blood.

The shooter vanished back into the alley.

"Son of a bitch!" Hayes yelled, swinging his rifle toward the retreating figure.

Then chaos erupted. Three men charged out of the ransacked dorm, wielding makeshift weapons. Teddy was shoved aside as they descended on Hayes. He barely registered the brick that smashed into Hayes' face, turning it into a grotesque mask. The officer fell, and the attackers set upon him, their blows relentless.

A teenage boy and a woman joined the fray, stomping on Wright's lifeless body. They rushed to strip the officers of their weapons.

One man, a rough-edged brute, glanced at Teddy. After a quick assessment, he jerked his head in a curt nod and muttered, "Better arm yourself. Things are about to turn ugly here."

Just as quickly as they had appeared, they scattered, leaving Teddy alone with the cold, the dead, and the echo of violence in the air.

So much for the easy way out of here.

An alarm wailed from the central control tower. Teddy wasn't sure if it was triggered by the chaos unfolding here or something else at the gallows. Either way, he knew he had to move fast.

Teddy crouched beside Hayes's body, quickly rifling through the vest's pockets. He found only a pack of stale cigarettes and a pair of handcuffs—hardly useful. Pleas for backup crackled through the officers' radios, but Teddy remained focused on reaching Ein before everything erupted into violence. He grabbed Hayes's FEMA pass card and yanked the radio from its holster, stuffing it in his back pocket as he stood. Then, with a deep breath, he sprinted towards the building perched atop the hill.

"Attention: due to terrorist activity, an emergency lockdown has been declared. All residents must remain in their dorms, or they will be detained."

The locks of every dormitory clicked simultaneously—a strange, ominous sound that echoed down the path. Teddy's pace quickened. Almost in direct response to the lockdown, civilians emerged from the alleys. Armed with blunt objects and a few rifles, they marched toward the gallows, fists raised, voices loud and angry.

"No food, no peace," they chanted. "You kill ours; we kill yours!"

The unexpected unity and coordination of these strangers, who only weeks ago were simply socializing around campfires, was remarkable.

Realizing he couldn't cut through the advancing crowd, Teddy veered off, running in the opposite direction. He rounded a corner too fast and skidded on the ice, but regained his footing. To his left, a line of troops blocked the pathway to the dining hall, shields and fiberglass batons ready. To his right, the swelling mob of civilians gathered near the gallows, hurling bricks, stones, and trash at the officers. These makeshift missiles flew overhead, bouncing harmlessly off shields or sinking into the snow.

As the troops advanced in tight formation, a secondary team fell in behind. A sergeant, megaphone in hand, shouted, "Disperse at once, or we will use force—"

His words were lost under the roar of the protesting crowd. Teddy, dodging small stones and bottles, ran toward the chaos. Tear gas canisters and smoke bombs arced over him, landing among the protesters and enveloping the area in a dense, choking fog. Many scattered, seeking clean air, while others, faces covered with makeshift masks, stumbled about in the haze, launching their projectiles wildly.

With his nose buried in the crook of his arm, Teddy pushed through the smoke. His eyes watered, his lungs burned, but he didn't slow down. Disoriented figures coughed and wheezed around him, shadows in the milky white fog. Finally breaking through to clearer air, Teddy caught his breath.

He stopped in front of the gallows to regroup. The crowd had retreated, leaving behind the twisted remains of Mayville and his men in the snow. Teddy wiped his eyes with his sleeve and squinted at the administrative building, now barely visible through the lingering smoke.

"So close, yet so far," he muttered to himself.

With the confrontation between the riot squad and the civilians intensifying, there was no way he'd be able to waltz inconspicuously up the main road; he'd have to find another way.

Teddy glanced down the footpath leading back to his dorm and saw a growing group of civilians. Fueled by desperation, they smashed random dormitory doors with large chunks of the gallows' wreckage, their peers cheering them on with a manic fervor. The intoxicating allure of lawlessness had gripped a population reduced to little more than unskilled labor.

Two burly men dragged an orderly out of a dorm, and the crowd descended on him with homicidal glee.

"Collaborating scum!" they yelled, stomping relentlessly until the life was crushed from his body.

Disgusted by the scene, Teddy turned his attention back to finding a way into the building where Ein was held. Just as he was about to give up, he spotted a narrow alley past the gallows—a path he'd explored weeks ago during his search for Ein. This alley, wedged between two warehouses, led to a lot near the motor pool's turnstiles, where the buses lined up for work calls. It was a direct route to the administration building.

As he started towards the alley, gunshots split the air. Teddy ducked and covered his head, but the gunfire wasn't aimed at him. The mob was firing at the troops.

A frantic voice erupted from the radio in his pocket: "Foxtrot to Jayhawk Control: civs are using firearms!"

A calmer voice responded, setting a grim tone: "Jayhawk Control to all units: use of lethal force is authorized. Fire at will."

What followed was immediate and brutal. Riot troops unleashed a barrage from their automatic rifles into the crowd. Screams echoed as people dropped their makeshift weapons, scrambling over each other to retreat. The troops advanced, ruthlessly firing at any movement. A few protestors, armed with small-caliber handguns or rifles looted from fallen officers, attempted to hold their ground, but the troops quickly singled them out and eliminated them.

Teddy sprinted across the courtyard and took cover behind what was left of the gallows. He got down and pressed his back against the wood, desperately sucking in air.

The protestors scattered, ducking and diving behind mounds of trash before they vanished down alleys and side streets. It took just a few minutes for the pathway to be empty of anyone except those wearing a uniform and the dead. The riot troops stopped firing, dropped their magazines, and reloaded as they looked around at their handiwork.

A sergeant keyed his mic and looked to the control tower. "Control, do you have a visual on the area?"

"Negative, Foxtrot. It's too saturated with chemical agents. We have no visual: over."

The sergeant stepped forward, raised his visor, and pointed to one of the alleys. "Break off in pairs and sweep all escape routes!"

Teddy peered around his makeshift cover, his heart pounding as he watched the troops spread out in tactical formation. His attention shifted abruptly to movement above. Through the lingering smoke, unnoticed by the sharp eyes in the tower and overlooked by the ground troops, figures appeared.

Atop the dormitory rooftops, at least thirty shrouded figures readied themselves. Each clutched a glass bottle. With swift, practiced movements, they lit their Molotov cocktails and hurled them down at the unsuspecting troops below.

What followed was chaos. Flames engulfed the entire battalion. Screams of agony and terror filled the air as soldiers dropped, flailing in the snow to extinguish the fires that consumed them. Some ran forward, arms thrashing, their body armor melting into their flesh. The ammunition in their tactical vests popped and crackled like sinister firecrackers.

Almost two agonizing minutes passed before silence fell over the scorched battlefield, ending the brutal spectacle. The once formidable riot battalion of Camp Jayhawk lay defeated, their bodies still as the surrounding flames dwindled.

As the rooftop assailants disappeared into the dissipating smoke, a group of protesters emerged from hiding on the ground, their cheers and whoops cutting through the somber air.

The previously calm voice on the radio in Teddy's pocket now cracked with urgency: "Jayhawk Control to remaining ground units: dormitory security is compromised. Lost contact with Foxtrot. Fall back to the administration cordon! Heavy armament squadron, move in and suppress all hostiles! Repeat: heavy armament contingency is a-go!"

Teddy sprinted down the narrow alley toward the motor pool, but came to an abrupt stop as he took in the scene before him.

A formidable force had assembled in front of the administration building, perched ominously on the hilltop. Rows of officers, rifles at the ready, formed a daunting line. Behind them, injured officers staggered uphill, seeking refuge behind this new line of defense. At the base, the vehicular sally port opened, releasing a convoy of Humvees, each mounted with .50 caliber machine guns, manned by officers in full armor. Three black FEMA SUVs, sirens blaring, followed closely.

Teddy's stomach knotted. Breaking through that line to reach Ein seemed impossible now. He considered retreating to regroup.

As he pondered his next move, a crowd of unruly protesters surged uphill, brandishing makeshift weapons. They didn't get far. The lead Humvee's gunner opened fire, and within seconds, tracer rounds transformed the advancing group into unrecognizable gory remains.

The convoy pressed forward, indifferent to the carnage it left behind. Small arms fire ricocheted off the armored vehicles as a handful of rebels took a desperate stand from a nearby rooftop. In response, the gunners targeted the building, unleashing a barrage that obliterated the structure. The roof caved, burying the rebels under a tomb of rubble.

The concussion of the blasts was deafening. Teddy turned and fled back toward the courtyard as the building collapsed around him. Concrete rained down, and he slipped across the icy terrain, tumbling back into the alley just as the building gave way.

Covered in dust and coughing, Teddy lurched back onto the main pathway. Civilians, terror-stricken, brushed past him, dropping their weapons and fleeing from the unstoppable advance of the armored convoy.

Teddy turned just in time to see a Humvee turn onto the pathway, the convoy in lethal pursuit.

"Oh, shit…" he gasped, and with adrenaline surging, he sprinted alongside the fleeing crowd, the gunners' relentless fire echoing behind him.

As Teddy fled, the surrounding crowd dwindled rapidly, victims of the indiscriminate gunfire. The footpath erupted in small explosions as bullets ricocheted off the concrete, sending chips flying from the nearby dorms. A man running alongside Teddy exploded in a gruesome burst like a smashed pomegranate, showering Teddy in blood and gore. The sound of the convoy's engines roared louder, ominously signaling their approach. Teddy felt like a target at a shooting range, fearfully awaiting the inevitable shot.

From a rooftop, a cloaked figure launched petrol bombs at the advancing convoy. The first bottle smashed against the lead vehicle, igniting a burst of flames across its windshield, yet it continued undeterred. The gunner promptly retaliated, turning his weapon towards the rooftop assailant. A burst of gunfire later, the figure plummeted to the street below, just as part of the building crumbled from the impact of the heavy rounds.

Seizing the momentary chaos as his chance, Teddy veered sharply right, darting down a narrow alley. Others tried to mimic his escape but weren't as quick; tracer rounds from the gunner's weapon cut them down, their bodies flung violently across the icy asphalt.

Emerging on the other side of the alley, Teddy found himself in a cramped service corridor squeezed between two rows of dormitories. Debris from demolished gambling huts and abandoned vendor stalls cluttered the path, making navigation treacherous. People were huddled among the rubble and behind the remnants of stalls, their faces etched with fear. Above him, on the rooftop of one of the dorms, Teddy noticed a trio armed with what appeared to be grenade launchers. They moved with agility, leaping from one roof to the next, keeping pace with the relentless convoy below.

Teddy couldn't help but think the rebels had some surprises stashed away as he spotted the launchers.

Yet, he remained skeptical. A few grenade launchers seemed insufficient to dent FEMA's formidable onslaught, especially considering the sheer number of troops stationed up at the administration building.

Navigating through the chaos, Teddy scrambled over the debris of a shattered shop and hurried down another alleyway. He emerged onto the main footpath leading back to his dorm. Given the dire circumstances, he decided to hold off on reaching Ein until the situation calmed down— maybe the coming nightfall and colder weather would dampen the fighting.

As he jogged toward his dorm, the extent of the destruction astounded him. Many dormitories had their doors busted open or propped up. Bodies of both officers and civilians peppered the snow, strewn and still. Some of the wounded, unable to walk, writhed and cried out for help as he passed.

Ahead, a young officer with short, red hair stumbled out of an alley. The man's rifle and helmet were missing; his wool balaclava had been pulled off. His broken nose contorted, and his dislocated jaw dangled, allowing his tongue to loll out grotesquely. Bruises bloomed across his battered face. Teddy slowed as he noticed the officer still weakly clutching a fiberglass baton, a look of defeat etched on his face. The officer glanced at Teddy, but seemed too dazed to care as he shuffled along the path. Giving the man a wide berth, Teddy then picked up his pace again.

Behind him, an explosion rattled the ground and sent windows shattering nearby. He wondered if that was the convoy meeting its end— had those grenade launchers done the trick after all?

The unmistakable, thunderous reply of the gunner's weapons answered his question.

When Teddy finally reached his dorm, he found Zoey pacing, her whimpers filling the tense air. She lowered her tail and ears, making her distress palpable even in the chaos that enveloped them.

"Zoey?" Teddy called out. "How did you get out?"

Zoey approached him, her usual vibrancy dampened, whimpering faintly. As Teddy noticed her fur matted with blood, a chill ran through him.

"Oh no…" he murmured under his breath.

Kneeling, he gently ran his fingers through her coat, searching for a wound. Zoey responded with a timid, sorrowful lick. Standing back up, Teddy was perplexed to find it wasn't her blood. As he approached the dorm, he saw the door had been forced open, much like the others.

"What happened, girl?"

Inside, the scene that unfolded was grim. Perry lay contorted on the floor. A horrifying sight. His red armband jutted from his mouth, mimicking a twisted tongue. Someone cruelly gouged out his eyes and his body bore multiple stab wounds.

Speechless, Teddy did the only thing he could—he fetched a sheet from an empty bunk and draped it over the body, his hands shaking. He watched, heart sinking, as blood seeped through the fabric, staining it crimson.

"I'm sorry…" he whispered, his voice barely audible.

Outside, the sound of gunfire intensified, mingling with the wail of approaching sirens. Teddy glanced at the open doorway where snow drifted in, creating a cold, ghostly veil. He knew he couldn't risk being seen; if an officer spotted him, it could be fatal.

"Come on, girl. Let's go hunker down somewhere until this passes," he said, his voice low and urgent.

He grabbed a couple of blankets and led Zoey into the communal showers. There, in the cramped, cold tile space, they huddled together. Teddy did what he had done for most of his adult life—waited.

18

Throughout the day, the incessant skirmishes between the rebels and the police rattled the thin walls of Teddy's hideout. The whine of small-caliber gunfire clashed with the mechanical thunder from the turret guns. Explosions, some close enough to dislodge plaster from the shower ceiling, shook the room, their violence echoed by the resounding boom of heavy artillery and mortar rounds.

Teddy listened, half-hoping the rebels were gaining ground, yet deep down, he recognized the futility. He remembered what he had once told Ein on the train: they'll never break us. Now, those words rang hollow. Anger and bravado could only carry a man so far against an armored battalion.

"Grit," he muttered to himself, a wry, humorless smile crossing his face. Hock's description of him seemed so inadequate now.

Turning his thoughts to something more constructive seemed the better path. He might not overthrow the regime, but he was determined to fulfill his promise to Ein, even if it meant risking his own life. It felt like a fool's errand, a desperate bid for redemption for dragging Jane and Danny into that disaster at the stadium.

But stepping out into a war zone unprepared was suicide.

Teddy had cleaned most of the blood from Zoey's coat. She seemed grateful, snuggling close, shivering slightly under the blankets they shared in the corner of the shower stall. Zoey's loyalty comforted him in a way only a dog's presence could; she seemed to understand his turmoil and stayed close, her body warmth mingling with his as he stroked her damp fur.

The chatter on the radio painted a vivid picture of the chaos outside. The rebels had compromised the armory early in the conflict, though

142

it seemed they had secured little beyond the launchers. While the convoy distracted itself with every moving target, another group of rebels raided the food storage warehouse, making off with supplies before the officers could regroup and respond. The loss of provisions didn't sit well with the police—several SUVs had raced off in pursuit, none returning to the fray.

Three dormitories were now smoldering ruins.

Gaps in the perimeter fences, hastily cut by escaping individuals, went unattended despite explicit orders to seal them. By afternoon, the situation worsened when a rocket struck the control tower, sending it crashing down. With the tower gone, the radio waves devolved into frantic, indecisive exchanges between Hock and his sergeants, each trying to assert control over the deteriorating situation.

Finally, a transmission crackled through the radio, a call sign Teddy didn't recognize. "USNORTHCOM hailing Jayhawk Command on all frequencies: we have no available units in your region to respond to your camp's distress beacon. Begin decampment protocols."

It was the last coherent message to filter through before the radio's battery surrendered to silence. The abrupt quiet sharpened Teddy's already frayed nerves. Restlessly, he rose several times—much to Zoey's chagrin—and peered into the dorm corridor, checking for any unwanted visitors.

As the day bled into evening, the sporadic gunfire dwindled until only intermittent shots punctuated the silence. By nightfall, all was quiet.

It would have been the ideal moment to venture out and assess the aftermath, but weariness and hunger weighed heavily on Teddy. As darkness enveloped them, he slumped against the cold tile, Zoey nestled against his side. Soon, both succumbed to exhaustion, drifting into a deep, uneasy sleep.

19

DECEMBER 20th, 2:41 A.M.

Teddy's eyes shot open at the sound of a distant train horn. He looked around the shower in a sleepy haze and saw Zoey alert and staring at him, ears perked. He rubbed the sleep from his eyes, and he realized he might have slept through his chance to operate under the cover of darkness.

In a rush, he threw off his blanket and scrambled to his feet. Peering through the open doorway, he sighed in relief to see it was still night.

Zoey wagged her tail and sidled up to him, her expression sweet and expectant, stirring a pang of guilt in Teddy. He hadn't even considered her in his plans.

"I'm sorry, girl, but you have to stay here," he told her.

She tilted her head, her eyes still fixed on him.

"I'm serious," he continued, his tone wavering. "You're on your own now. I'm sorry—really."

Zoey's ears drooped at the sound of his words, and she let out a soft whimper. Teddy ran a hand over his face, then let out a heavy sigh.

"Fine, girl…you win." He zipped his jacket, checked for the FEMA access card in his pocket, and motioned to the door. "Come on."

Zoey's demeanor brightened immediately, and she barked happily as she trotted alongside him.

Outside, the cold was more biting than before. The melted snow had refrozen, creating a hazardous sheet of ice on the footpaths, and large icicles dangled ominously from the rooftops. Though the camp's high-mast lamps were off, the full moon cast a harsh, pale light over the desolate scene.

Teddy stopped short at the sight of hundreds of bodies frozen and half-buried in the ice. "Dear God…"

As they moved further, the devastation from the day's conflicts was stark. Entire dormitories lay in ruins, while others flickered with the eerie orange glow of unchecked fires. Bullet-riddled guard towers stood abandoned, their searchlights shattered. Black smoke billowed from the ruins atop the concrete pillar where Jayhawk Control once stood.

Teddy cautiously walked on the icy path, struck by the extent of the collapse. Zoey stayed close, her nose brushing against the frozen corpses, her ears low and tail flat.

A few shell-shocked civilians scavenged the dead for supplies, but scattered at his approach. He thought about reaching out to them, but dismissed the idea. What could they possibly offer him now? Given what they'd been through, he figured anyone still alive and sane was lucky.

They skirted around the charred remains of a Humvee, its frame crumpled against a dormitory and reduced to a skeletal husk. Teddy hadn't seen any other vehicles patrolling and wondered if the authorities had given up the search or written everyone off as casualties.

A train horn blared again; he jumped and turned toward the jarring noise.

"Those idiots are still bringing people here?" he asked aloud.

A morbid answer formed in his mind. *Yes, but this time they're bringing cops…and lots of guns.* He shuddered, knowing that by now they had likely abandoned the remaining civilians to fend for themselves against the cold and hunger. Either the train was passing through, or the conductor was oblivious to the fact that the Walls of Jericho had crumbled and chaos reigned supreme.

In the distance, the administration building stood untouched atop its hill, its lights blazing like a beacon in the night, every rooftop halogen floodlight glaring down at the frozen landscape below. Teddy maneuvered around a mass of concrete debris that blocked most of the path.

Turning to Zoey, he flashed a weary smile. "We're almost there, girl."

She barked in response and wagged her tail.

As the footpath widened into the main passageway that stretched from the train station to the administration building, Teddy paused, taking cover at the corner to survey the area. He held out a hand, signaling Zoey to stay put; obediently, she paused.

Some sections of the chain-link fence that bordered the perimeter were intact, except where vehicles had flattened entire sections. A FEMA SUV sat on flat tires beside an overturned Humvee, its olive paint scorched away. The gates of the vehicular sally port stood open, and

Teddy watched as three military flatbeds rolled out of the camp, loaded with officers and crates of supplies. In the distance, the taillights of four more trucks faded as they sped down the dirt road, their beds crammed with officers clinging to the sides.

"That's right. Cut and run, motherfuckers," Teddy said, a bitter smile crossing his lips.

His gaze shifted back to the hill, his heart sinking as he observed a skeleton crew of officers coordinating an evacuation. They ushered a procession of researchers and nurses out of the administration building towards the waiting Amtrak train at the intake dock. The medical and research staff, laden with boxes of documents, still wore their biohazard suits, though their hoods and respirators were absent. Teddy searched for Ein or any of the other human test subjects but saw none, concluding that they, too, had been left behind.

"We'll wait for them to finish and then get the hell out of here," Teddy told Zoey as he ducked back under cover and leaned against the wall. Zoey affectionately licked the back of his hand; Teddy playfully shooed her away. "It's too cold for all that, girl. Your drool's gonna give me frostbite."

She barked with glee, her body wiggling, eager to play, but the timing and place were all wrong. Teddy crouched down to calm her, placing a finger to his lips and gently shushing her. Undeterred, she barked again, tail whipping back and forth.

One of the escorting officers halted. "You hear that?"

His companion paused and pivoted toward the sound. "Could be another roach trying to take a shot at us. Let's check it out."

The two officers activated their tactical flashlights and started in Teddy's direction while the rest continued shepherding the medical staff towards the train.

Zoey's playful demeanor vanished as she sensed the danger. A low growl emerged from deep within her throat, her fur bristling along her back. Teddy risked a quick glance around the corner and saw the officers advancing with their weapons drawn.

"Shit." He patted Zoey quickly. "Come on, girl, we gotta go."

They turned sharply, retreating the way they had come, Zoey's paws churning up the snow. Their movement didn't go unnoticed.

"Movement!" one officer called out. "Someone's back there!"

Both officers started running. Teddy squeezed between a pile of concrete debris and a dorm and shimmied through as fast as he could manage. Zoey clambered up and over the pile and scurried ahead of Teddy. She turned toward him and bared her teeth, growling as the officers neared. Teddy pressed through the passageway and headed toward one of the open dormitory doors.

He waved at Zoey. "Come on!"

An earlier mortar strike had wreaked havoc on the dorm, blasting a large hole in the roof and carving a gaping crater in the floor. Mangled civilian corpses were strewn around the crater, some hanging halfway into it. Teddy took cover behind an overturned bunk, pressing his back against the steel. He pulled Zoey close and held her tightly against his chest.

He leaned down and whispered in her ear. "Easy, girl, just be quiet."

Zoey kept her head low and sniffed the air zealously. She didn't try to pull away, but her body remained tense, ready to spring at a moment's notice. Judging by how violently she reacted every time she saw the uniforms, Teddy wondered if one of the officers had lashed out at her during the unrest.

Teddy stroked her back to calm her, but it didn't seem to have much effect, so he whispered, "Easy."

"Split up and check the dorms," one of the men said outside the door. "I'll take the right, you take left."

"Got it," the other responded.

"Watch your ass. I guarantee they're armed."

One of the officers stepped inside and scanned the room cautiously with his rifle's tactical light. The wooden planks creaked under his boots. Teddy remained motionless, with his arm around Zoey. He could smell the cordite clinging to the man's uniform as he got closer.

Please, just go away.

The officer slipped past the bunk where Teddy was hiding and kept walking. He reached the end of the dorm, swept the inside of the communal shower with his light, and then lowered his weapon.

"We're clear in here!" he shouted.

As soon as the officer turned, he locked eyes on Teddy, who sat motionless with his back against the bunk and Zoey in his arms. The officer's eyes widened, and he jumped back, terrified. All he emitted was a high-pitched whimper as he swung his weapon back around.

"Easy!" Teddy exclaimed. "I'm unarmed! I was looking for Hock!"

In a blur, Zoey leaped from Teddy's arms and charged. She launched herself forcefully, her front paws slamming into the man's chest as she clamped her jaws around his throat. The officer reacted instinctively, pulling the trigger as he flailed and fell backward. His rifle spat out rounds, the shots piercing the roof and ricocheting off the lockers, missing their intended target.

Zoey's grip only tightened, her teeth sinking deeper as crimson blood flowed. The man scrambled, trying desperately to dislodge her, but she was relentless. He collapsed onto his back, his gun slipping from his grasp. He thrashed under Zoey's weight, his hands beating against her in vain, but she maintained her hold, shaking her head fiercely.

The man's eyes rolled back in their sockets. His arms and legs went limp and his head slumped back. His body's final, undignified act was the release of his bladder.

Finally, Zoey released him. She stepped off the now-still body and trotted back to Teddy, her tongue and muzzle stained with blood.

Teddy, stunned at the savagery he had just witnessed, looked over at the dead man, who lay just feet away in a puddle of his own blood and piss. He turned back to Zoey and stroked the side of her head with a trembling hand.

"Good girl…"

Zoey, seemingly unaware of the uneasiness in his voice, happily barked in response and wagged her tail.

A light shone into the dorm as the other officer stepped into the doorway. The beam focused on the man's mauled corpse on the floor. He gasped and took a step back.

"Sweet Jesus!"

Zoey's grin vanished, and her hackles rose again. She snarled and bolted from behind the bunk, charging at the officer. The officer hastily aimed his rifle and fired, but his shots only splintered the wooden floor. Zoey lunged at him, her mouth agape, ready to strike.

He fired again, and Zoey yelped in pain as a round tore through her right hind leg. She floundered in the air and landed against the man's chest. The officer stumbled backward and landed on the snow with a yelp. Zoey tumbled off of him, rolled back onto her feet, and darted away down the footpath, hobbling on three legs.

"Nasty bitch!" the man snarled.

He quickly got back on his feet, pointed his rifle at her, and fired again. He was so focused on the task at hand that he didn't see the burly brute approach him. Teddy knocked the rifle's barrel up toward the sky and drove his fist against the side of the man's head as hard as he could.

The officer's helmet flew off of his head and the lower portion of his jaw snapped to the side. He turned to his assailant in a bewildered daze. Teddy spun the man around and wrapped his arm around the man's throat in a tight chokehold. He pulled the officer inside the dorm. The officer rasped for breath as he clawed at the forearm that had his throat in a crushing grip. He kicked his legs out and tried to twist and worm away; the thought of using his holstered sidearm apparently never even occurred to him as anxiety trumped reason.

Teddy gritted his teeth, and he broke out in sweat even though the temperature was well below freezing. He closed his eyes and squeezed tighter than he thought possible.

There was a sickening snap, and the officer's body suddenly went limp.

Teddy let the dead officer slump to the ground, stepping over the body to retrieve the fallen rifle. Outside, he surveyed the pathway and adjacent alleys—desolate and silent. No threats lingered in the immediate darkness.

He switched off the tactical light and cradled the rifle, his gaze falling on the blood-speckled snow. The trail of crimson drops led him down the footpath to where Zoey stood, cradling her injured leg against her body. Her ears perked up, and she seemed to smile at him despite the pain she must've been in.

Teddy felt a smile tug at his own lips as he waved to her. "Come here, girl. You did well."

Teddy was disheartened, but he couldn't really blame her. His travel companions never seemed to fare well, so he figured she was making a smarter decision than most humans would. He turned and headed back to the dorm to plan his next move. Still, the realization did nothing to ease the sting of her departure.

Resigned, Teddy turned back toward the dorm to plan his next steps. Entering the administration building would require more than just stealth and a pass card—especially since some officers had stayed behind, complicating matters further.

He glanced down at the dead officer, anger flaring briefly. He unleashed a few swift kicks at the body. "Prick."

As he paused, breathing heavily, his eyes assessed the officer's gear and uniform. They were roughly the same size. A grim opportunity presented itself, and Teddy realized he had something far more useful than a pass card.

20

The fit wasn't as close as he had hoped. His legs felt like overstuffed sausages in the black BDU pants, and his crotch felt like someone was working him over with a monkey wrench.

Despite those shortcomings, everything else fit well. He had ample room in the shirt—*thanks, malnutrition*—and the padded armor fit perfectly after he made some minor adjustments to the nylon straps. He found nothing particularly useful in the uniform's many tactical pockets, but he found a pocketknife and an extra magazine loaded with thirty rounds.

Decked out in full FEMA officer regalia and carrying an assault rifle, Teddy marched up the hill. He strode past two sentries and into the lobby of the administration building without attracting a single suspicious glance. A balaclava obscured the lower half of his face, and his riot helmet was slightly tilted to hood his eyes.

Hell, if he knew it would've been that easy, he would've tried it weeks ago.

Smoke hung in the lobby as the fire alarms emitted a piercing, ceaseless wail and the emergency strobes flashed. Strips of shredded paper covered the floor, and bullet-riddled computers were piled in front of the reception desk.

A voice came through the Motorola clipped to his duty belt. "Alpha-Ten to Command: be advised, sanitization protocols are underway. Completion time is estimated at twenty minutes: over."

Hock responded, "Command to Alpha-Ten: I suggest you hurry it up. I don't like sitting out here in the open. If anything pops off outside, we're moving out—with you or without you. Copy?"

"Uh…" The voice hesitated. "Ten-four, Command, we'll, uh, make it fast: over."

"I guess I better hurry, too," Teddy said as he neared the elevators.

The silver doors slid open, and an officer, helmet-free and chuckling, escorted two coughing researchers into the lobby. As he passed Teddy, the officer rapped his knuckles on Teddy's helmet.

"Relax, man, there aren't any roaches in here—just eggheads! You don't need to march around like you're ready for war."

Teddy forced a laugh, the tension tight in his chest as he quickly slipped into the elevator. He fumbled with the pass card, tapping it against the reader and then jabbing at the close button repeatedly.

"Can never be too careful, I reckon."

Just as the officer turned, alerted by Teddy's unfamiliar voice, the doors slid shut, sealing Teddy inside. He exhaled a heavy sigh of relief and leaned against the wall.

"Attention: priority alert," a voice announced over the intercom, "an emergency has occurred. All staff are required to evacuate the facility immediately."

The elevator descended rapidly, opening to a corridor clouded with thick, black smoke. Shredded paper carpeted the floor like confetti, and the dimmed lights flickered, barely sustained by the backup generators. The piercing wail of the fire alarm echoed incessantly down the passageway. Teddy pressed forward, his breathing labored, his eyes stinging—aware of the deadly threat of smoke inhalation.

As he hurried past long windows looking into office areas, he saw officers donned in gas masks feverishly shredding stacks of documents. Nearby, another group violently smashed computer terminals with sledgehammers and fire axes.

Passing another set of windows, Teddy saw two figures in silver flame-retardant suits and hooded respirators in the middle of a lab. Equipped with chemical flamethrowers, they methodically scorched everything in sight. Glass beakers frothed and shattered under the intense heat, a sealed freezer burst open, and racks of test tubes exploded like firecrackers. Within moments, months of research and experimentation were reduced to molten glass and charred remains—a desperate attempt to erase all traces of their clandestine activities.

Nothing to see here, folks—keep moving, pass go, collect $200.

Teddy shook his head and kept moving. He passed three other sets of laboratories—all of which had been blackened and destroyed by flames—before turning a corner and passing through a set of double doors that led to the observation bay. Ahead of him, three white-suits carrying submachine guns headed toward the bay's door. Gatsby stood at the far end of the hall with his hands extended toward the white-suits. Soot covered his lab coat.

"Please, don't! I implore you! You're ruining everything!"

The white-suits kept walking. One said, "We have our orders, Doc."

"At least allow me to take some of their blood for research before you do what you're about to do!" Gatsby shouted. "You owe me that much!"

"Orders are orders. Just stand back!" a white-suit commanded.

Teddy started walking down the hall, weapon ready. One of the white-suits turned as he approached.

"What are you doing down here, soldier?" he asked. "If you're here to help with the test subjects, then you should know that you can't enter the room without the proper PPE."

Teddy kept moving forward but quickened his pace. The other two white-suits stopped and turned.

One of them raised a hand and shooed him away. "You can't go in with us! They're infectious!"

Teddy raised his rifle and pulled the trigger repeatedly as he swept the weapon from side to side. The white-suits shuddered violently as the bullets ripped through them and formed red splotches across their protective fabric. Gatsby ducked and covered his head.

Teddy stopped and watched as the white-suits collapsed, then focused his attention on the doctor and started walking forward again.

Gatsby paled as he raised his hands above his head in a sign of surrender. "Have you gone crazy?"

"Crazy?" Teddy asked as he reached up and pulled the balaclava down to reveal the lower portion of his face. "That's rich, coming from you."

Gatsby's eyes widened, and he trembled as soon as he recognized Teddy. He swallowed hard and took a few cautious steps back. His eyes danced anxiously between Teddy and the patients in the observation bays.

"What are you going to do?"

"The right thing," Teddy said.

He took his pass card and pressed it against the scanner. A light above the door flashed green, and a hydraulic locking mechanism unlatched.

"You can't!" Gatsby shouted, his brow furrowed. "They're all carriers! Just one of those individuals has enough viral load to take down an entire settlement! I've already explained this to you, goddamnit!"

"And I've already explained that I think you're full of shit," Teddy said as he cracked the door open.

The sealed room gave a loud hiss as it sucked in new air.

"No!" Gatsby screamed. "Don't!"

His gaze darted down to one of the submachine guns that the white-suits had dropped and sprinted toward it. Teddy pointed his weapon and fired. Gatsby's body convulsed as bullets struck him. He landed hard against the tile and left a bloody smear as he slid to a stop in the middle of the corridor. He gave one last raspy breath, twitched, and then lay still.

Just as Teddy pulled the door all the way open, a second alarm started blaring and a robotic voice announced, "Attention: biohazard warning. Containment door opened without proper pressurization protocols. Environment compromised."

He ignored the recording and stepped inside of the observation bay. The people inside cowered against the wall and stared at Teddy's rifle, but Ein stepped forward with an elated, disbelieving expression on his tired face.

"You actually came…"

Teddy smiled at Ein, nodded, and then turned his attention toward the others. "Listen, I'm not here to hurt any of you, but the people I just shot most certainly were here to do you harm. You need to leave this place. There are more of them waiting outside and a few are armed. It's risky, but this is your only chance to get out of here; take it and give them hell." When the people in the group looked at each other doubtfully, he bellowed, "Go!"

They ran past him and out into the corridor, stopping only to pick up the weapons that the white-suits had dropped before scattering off in every direction.

"I'm glad to see that you're in one piece," Teddy said. He looked down at the tattooed datamatrix code on Ein's hand. Poor kid: he couldn't even imagine what sort of hell he had been subjected to in the name of science. When he looked up at his face, he noticed Ein was staring at him with a bewildered grin. "Why are you staring at me like that?"

Ein shook his head. "I just…can't believe it. How did you get down here? And why are you dressed like a cop?"

"It's a long fucking story. It went to hell up there, kid," Teddy said. "I'm just happy to see that you're—"

Ein stepped forward and gave him a hug. He closed his eyes as tears ran down his cheeks. "Thank you."

Teddy was taken aback. He awkwardly returned the hug and patted his back. "It's nothing, really. I promised you, didn't I?" He broke away and grinned. "Now, how about we get the hell out of here?"

Ein nodded and wiped his tears away with the back of his hand. "How are we going to do that, exactly?"

Teddy looked over at Gatsby's corpse lying in a growing pool of blood—specifically his clothes. "What size pants do you wear?"

Ein thought for a moment and then shook his head. "I have no clue anymore."

"Well, I guess it doesn't matter since we don't have many options," Teddy said. "Do you mind a little blood?"

"Can't stand it."

"Then you're really going to hate this next part."

21

Teddy stood in the elevator with Ein as it ascended. The balaclava obscured his face once more, and he kept his eyes hidden by the helmet's visor. His rifle was slung over his shoulder, and he kept one arm wrapped around Ein to help him stand.

Ein wore Gatsby's bloody lab coat and slacks, which fit him about as well as clown pants would. Bits of blood were dabbed on his face and he slicked back his long, scraggily hair with it. He slouched forward, grimaced, and pressed his tattooed hand against the elevator wall.

"Keep that hand in your pocket or they'll spot you right away," Teddy said.

"Sorry, but I think I'm going to hurl," Ein groaned as he stuffed his tattooed hand back in his coat pocket. "These clothes smell like blood and piss."

Teddy chuckled. "You look green about the gills, but that only adds to the disguise."

"Was all of this necessary?"

"Since they didn't have a closet full of fresh lab coats, I'd say that beggars can't be choosers."

Ein sighed. "It's not even very convincing."

"Don't sell yourself short," Teddy said. "You look pretty fucked up."

"That's what I'm talking about." Ein gestured at the bloody clothes. "I have these theatrics going on, but not a single wound. It looks fake."

"I could knock a few of your teeth out if you're going for an authentic look," Teddy teased.

"Hardy-har-har."

"Seriously—relax, kid. Everything will be fine. People aren't going to do much scrutinizing. They'll see the blood and that'll be enough for

155

them. Besides, with all those people from the observation rooms running around, those cops are going to have other things to worry about soon enough."

Ein looked skeptical. "Are you sure about that? They all seemed to be headed in different directions."

"There's nowhere for them to run, really." Teddy shrugged. "They'll cross paths soon enough. It's probably a good thing we got off of that floor before they did."

As if to illustrate Teddy's point, gunshots echoed from the floor below.

A voice shouted over the radio, "Alpha-Ten to Command: we're under civilian fire!"

Hock responded, "Alpha Command to Alpha-Ten: what civilians? We're monitoring your perimeter, and nobody came in."

"Negative, Command. Hostiles came from inside the facility! They're wearing hospital gowns!"

"Alpha-Ten, those are the test subjects! Neutralize them!"

The gunshots continued.

"Command, our security contingent got ambushed. We need backup!"

"Copy, Alpha-Ten. I'll send what I have from the train. Hold them off and do not let them escape or it will be your ass!"

"See?" Teddy said. "Problems of their own."

The lift came to a stop, and the doors slid open. Teddy kept an arm around Ein and led him through the empty lobby. A squadron of breathless officers came barreling through the front doors with their rifles at the ready.

"What the hell is going on down there?" one of them asked Teddy.

"Damn roaches," Teddy said. "Some white-suit fucked up royally and let them out. Now they're killing everyone!" He pointed at Ein. "This one is lucky that I got him out in one piece."

"Take him to the train with the others."

"Already on it," Teddy said.

The squad brushed past them and gathered around the elevator so they could cram themselves inside.

"Roaches?" Ein whispered once there was a respectable distance between them and the officers.

Teddy shrugged. "Long story."

They walked out the front doors and onto the snowy footpath. The biting cold struck both of them immediately.

"Christ, man. I'm freezing my ass off over here!" Ein exclaimed, teeth chattering.

"Welcome to winter in the Midwest," Teddy said.

"The Midwest?" Ein asked as he looked around.

"Yeah…Kansas."

Ein stared at him, clearly puzzled. "How do you know so—?"

"Also a long story," Teddy said.

As they trudged through the snow toward the Amtrak, Ein surveyed the battered camp with awe. "This place looks so different from when we arrived that night. What happened? How did everything go sideways?"

Teddy sighed. "Kid, once we're away from this place, I'll tell you every boring detail. Right now, let's focus on putting some miles between us and FEMA, yeah?"

At the bottom of the hill, they stopped in the clearing between the administration building and the train platform. There was a large section of flattened chain-link fence, but not a single drivable vehicle in sight.

"Shit. So much for the motor pool idea," Teddy muttered. He glanced around once more before setting his sights on the portion of the flattened fence. "It looks like we'll have to walk."

"In this weather?" Ein asked. "Are you crazy? We'll be dead by sunrise!"

Teddy rolled his eyes. "Do you have a better idea?"

"Yeah, actually, I do." Ein nodded toward the waiting train.

Teddy scoffed. "So we should saddle up with a bunch of cops and ride off where? To another camp?"

"All I know is that it's a better idea than walking." Ein jabbed a thumb up to the administration building. "Besides, it looked to me like all the cops went up the hill."

Teddy considered it and then conceded with a nod. "You make a good point. If there's nothing but a bunch of doctors and nurses on that train, then there isn't much of a threat." He looked at the train and then shrugged. "Fuck it. Let's go."

They navigated the icy terrain and climbed the wooden steps onto the train's loading platform. The train, once a regular Amtrak passenger liner, had been retrofitted with tinted windows shielded by protective steel mesh. Bullet holes and graffiti marred the length of every car.

Ein grinned. "Reminds me of the trains I used to see when I visited my buddy up in Newark."

"Yeah, this thing looks like it's been through hell and back a few times," Teddy remarked. "It must've been taken through some rough areas, but that doesn't surprise me."

"Why's that?"

"Because I know firsthand that things aren't much better outside of these little FEMA camps."

Ein raised a brow. "How would you know? Have you been?" When Teddy merely stared back, Ein rolled his eyes. "Let me guess. It's a long story. Right?"

"Right." Teddy led him toward one of the passenger car's open doors. "Now, be quiet, act injured, keep that tattoo in your pocket, and try to keep your head down. Chances are that one of these scientists will remember one test subject with purple tips."

"Got it."

"What's the deal with that, anyway?"

"The deal with what?"

"That hair," Teddy said. "What made you dye it purple in the first place?"

Ein gave him a wily grin. "It's a long story."

Inside the passenger car, boxes of documents and office trinkets hastily tossed into trash bags occupied most of the seats. Weary researchers and medical staff members scattered throughout the carriage, with not a single officer in sight.

Teddy leaned closer to Ein's ear. "Let's make our way to the locomotive."

"Why?" Ein whispered back.

"Because we're hijacking it."

They walked through the enclosed gangway connections and passed through the carriages on their way to the front of the train. They encountered only a handful of medical staff members, and they all looked nearly asleep on their feet. Nobody paid them any mind, so Teddy let go of Ein and the two men walked normally. The last two passenger carriages they passed through were empty.

"This is almost too easy," Teddy said with a grin as they entered the gangway that led into the dining car. "We're near the front."

"What are we going to do about them?" Ein asked.

"Who?"

"Them," Ein emphasized as he pointed back the way they came. "We're just going to take them with us?"

"If the coupler isn't under too much tension, they're staying and we're leaving," Teddy said.

Ein looked puzzled. "What is that supposed to mean?"

Teddy opened the gangway doors and peeked into the dining car. The seats around the tables were empty, yet the main aisle was cluttered with boxes of ammunition and stacks of military equipment.

"Perfect."

Ein stared at him with a puzzled expression. "What are you going on about, old man?"

"Watch and see, kid."

Teddy closed the doors and retrieved the knife from his pocket, flicked open the blade, and drove it into the gangway's rubber seal. He brought the blade down and tore a large hole in the membrane; cold air whistled through the gap.

"What the hell, man?" Ein shivered, wrapped his arms around his chest, and stepped back as Teddy pulled apart the rubber and lifted the padded steel walkway panels. "Are you nuts?"

"Just trust me."

Teddy pulled back another protective layer of flooring and exposed the carriage's coupler mechanism. He got down on his stomach and lifted the cut lever with both hands, grunting. The compressed air line let out a rush of air as the coupling heads separated. The locking pin disengaged, and the knuckle turned. Behind Teddy and Ein, the passenger carriages went dark.

Teddy stood up, dusted himself off, and gave Ein a smug smile with his arms extended. "Ta-da!"

Ein whistled and clapped his hands. "Impressive. Where did you learn how to do that?"

"When I was younger, I helped my old man with his cattle. A couple of times a year, we herded them from the ranch to the city. Well, actually, it was a podunk country town, but to me, Brownsville, Texas, felt like a big city. I loved those trips," Teddy chuckled as he closed the knife and tucked it back into his pocket. "We'd spend all day at the train yard, helping to load the cattle onto the stock cars. I learned a lot of useful stuff, though I never really did much with it."

"It came in handy tonight."

"Yeah, I reckon it did." He heard agitated voices coming from the passenger cars and frowned. "Let's get to the front and roll out of here before those eggheads ask somebody who turned off the lights."

They walked through the dining car and passed the gangway into the first-class cabin. Unlike the other empty carriages, commissioned officers in dress uniforms occupied many of the plush leather seats. Hock sat in the front row.

Once Teddy realized that the carriage was full of whatever was left of the upper echelon of the camp's command, his stomach dropped. He stopped and held out a hand to signal to Ein that he should do the same.

"Back out slowly," he whispered.

The door in the carriage's front opened, and a man wearing a dress uniform adorned with sergeant major insignias walked down the aisle while flipping through a folder full of films. He looked up at Ein, and then his gaze fell to his hands. Teddy's skin erupted in goose bumps as soon as he noticed that Ein's hands were out of his pockets and that his tattoo was visible, but it was too late to do anything about it.

The sergeant major's eyes widened at the sight of the datamatrix code; he leaped back and sent the flimsies flying. "That's one of the test subjects; he's infectious!"

The other officers jumped from their seats and stared at them with steely-eyed horror. A few fumbled with their pistols as they attempted to free them from their holsters, while Teddy shoved Ein aside, pointed his rifle at the crowd, and fired. Bullets darkened overhead light strips and shattered windows as they tore through seats and rebounded off the walls.

The sergeant major flew back as gunfire struck him down. Four of the other officers jolted before slumping to the floor. They never even cleared their holsters. At the front of the carriage, Hock ducked down and retreated through the gangway unscathed.

Teddy's gun clicked as he fired the last round. He ducked behind the seat across from him and hurriedly reloaded. Ein took cover behind a seat, covering his head with his hands. The three remaining officers drew their pistols and opened fire. Their shots chewed through the tops of the leather seats, sending wads of foam fluttering through the air like snow. As the cordite thickened in the air, Ein got on his belly and slid under the chair into the next row.

"Stay covered!" Teddy shouted above deafening tinnitus, but the kid either didn't listen or couldn't hear him. He peeked briefly around the corner, but quickly pulled back as bullets whistled past his head. "Goddamnit!"

Ein had continued working his way under the seats and advancing down the rows until he came across one of the slain officers. He pulled the pistol out of the man's holster and started firing from under the seat. Two officers howled as bullets took out their shins. They dropped their weapons and collapsed against the seats, struggling to hold themselves up. The last standing officer, a corporal, pointed his gun toward the back of the carriage and fired recklessly at the seats.

Teddy popped up and fired at the corporal, who flew back and flipped over the top seat, then bled out on the floor. The other two officers, their pistols spent, tried to crawl away, but were each taken down by three-round bursts to their backs.

Several brass casings clattered across the floor, and then a thick silence filled the room.

Teddy stepped out into the aisle and scanned the seats for any movement before lowering his rifle. "I think we're good."

Ein crawled out and stood with the pistol still in his hand. He reached his hand up and cupped his ear; blood trickled out from his earlobe and down his cheek.

"I think I'm deaf in one ear now."

"Probably just ruptured an eardrum. Mine are ringing, too. You'll be fine in a month or two," Teddy said, even though he didn't know how factual his diagnosis was. "You did good."

The train jolted them forward as it started to move. Panicked voices came from the radio.

"Where are you going? Wait!"

Cries of protest continued, but Hock didn't respond.

Ein stared out of the window as the train picked up speed and left the camp behind. "Where do you think it's headed?"

"Nowhere that we want to go. We need to get to the locomotive and take control of this thing." Teddy readied his rifle once more and started walking ahead. "Let's go—I saw Hock sneak into the next car. Watch your back."

They stepped over the corpses and passed through the gangway into the baggage carriage. The lights were dimmed, and cold air whistled through narrow window slits that ran along the roof. Refrigerated crates with the biohazard symbol on them were tethered to the floor with yellow nylon straps. Fog hung low around the crates' condensers and obscured the view ahead.

Ein stared at one of the crates as they passed. "What are these things for?"

"It looks like they were trying to move their science project to another location." Teddy squinted and carefully scanned the area with his rifle as he crept ahead. "Forget about that for now; focus on your surroundings."

"I can't see shit. Do you think he's in here?"

"I'd wager he's inside, waiting for us." Teddy heard Ein stop walking. "Come on, hurry up."

Ein remained silent.

"Kid?" Teddy asked.

"You came a long way just to die," Hock said.

Teddy spun toward the voice and raised his rifle.

Hock stood behind Ein with a pistol pressed against the back of the young man's head, glaring at Teddy with steely eyes and a flat expression. "Drop the guns."

Ein threw his pistol on the floor and raised his hands. Teddy kept his rifle aimed at Hock.

"Sanders, I thought you had mettle, but now I see you're just another short-sighted, selfish prick," Hock said.

"Let the kid go." Teddy's grip on the rifle tightened.

"Your attachment to this walking petri dish illustrates my point perfectly." Hock shook his head. "You know he's infectious, yet you still want to take him out into the world. Which settlement are you taking him to?" He chuckled. "I guess it doesn't matter. He'll kill off every one of them just by breathing."

"He's not sick," Teddy said, his eyes narrowing as his finger trembled lightly on the trigger. "If you're buying into that doctor's desperate scramble for relevance, then you're a goddamn fool. He's just grasping at straws, looking for funding or protection."

Hock stared impassively at him. "As obnoxious as Gatsby was, he knew what he was doing. The kid is sick."

"You don't know that!" Teddy shouted. "Hell, even he wasn't completely sure!"

"It's an unacceptable risk."

The train's speed increased, and the carriage rattled as it plowed through snowy tracks. Teddy wobbled and nearly fell, but he braced himself against the side of a biohazard crate, keeping his rifle leveled at the lieutenant with his finger steady on the trigger. Hock spread his feet for stability and kept the barrel of his pistol pressed firmly against the back of Ein's head.

"Just stop this train and let us walk away!" Teddy growled over the rumble of the carriage. "You'll never see us again."

"I can't do that," Hock said as he kept the pistol steady in his hand.

"Why?" Teddy asked. "Nobody will know. We sure as hell aren't going to tell anybody!"

Hock peered at him through narrowed eyes. "I have my orders, too, you know." He pointed at the containers. "We're working on a cure. It's a solution to a problem much larger than you and I. When we arrive at the next camp, we'll restore order once again."

"What does that have to do with letting us go?" Teddy asked in aggravation.

"It's simple. We're trying to cure the disease, but you're intent on spreading it," Hock said. "I'm sorry, but this is for—"

Suddenly, the carriage jolted violently, throwing everyone off balance.

Teddy grasped at the container to steady himself. Ein was less fortunate, slipping and sliding across the floor. Hock stumbled backward, his hand accidentally squeezing the trigger of his gun as he tried to regain his balance. The shot rang out, blasting a hole in the ceiling. He crashed against the wall, then quickly pressed his back to it, trying to regroup.

Teddy swung the rifle back up and took his shot.

Hock let out a croaking gasp as the bullets peppered his chest and sullied most of his decorative military regalia. Blood poured out of his wounds and down the front of his shirt. Teddy took cover behind the container and peeked over the top, training his rifle on Hock to fire a second round.

But there was no need.

Hock dropped his pistol and gave a few final raspy breaths. His startled gaze went down to his chest. He fell to his knees and, as his eyes glazed over, he looked at Teddy with something that resembled relief.

Teddy watched as the lieutenant fell face down and lay still. Only then did he lower his rifle, get to his feet, and turn to Ein.

"Are you okay?"

Ein scooted away from the corpse and then looked up at Teddy, nodding sheepishly.

Teddy extended a hand to help him up. "Come on. Let's go."

They walked through the gangway and came to a riveted steel door labeled, Stop: no access. Teddy pulled up the red hydraulic lever, and the door swung open. Bitter wind and pieces of ice whistled through the open doorway as the locomotive sped across frozen plains under a blanket of stars.

Ein backed away and shielded his squinted eyes with his forearm. "What gives?" he shouted over the engine noise. "There's no way to the cockpit?"

"There's a way, but this isn't a damn airplane!" Teddy bellowed back as he gripped onto the doorframe. He pointed to a narrow catwalk that wrapped around the locomotive. "We have to walk around to the front of this thing."

Ein appeared nauseated by the very idea of it. He looked over the edge at the bobbing coupler and the dangling chain as it struck the tracks below and threw up showers of sparks. He pulled back quickly.

"We're going too fast!"

"If we don't fall, we'll be fine." Teddy wasn't sure that his words brought him much comfort, but he really didn't have time to argue the point. "There's no other way! If we wait for the train to stop, we'll be at another camp and neither one of us wants that."

Ein frowned, but he didn't protest. Teddy stood at the edge of the doorway and looked down at the catwalk ahead. It was about a five-foot jump, with no room for errors. He removed some of his bulky riot armor and helmet to lighten his load. Reluctantly, he placed his rifle on the ground. He took a couple of steps back and took a running leap across the gap, but crashed onto the catwalk and went tumbling toward the opening. He grabbed one of the handrail's bars just in time. His heart thumped madly, and his whole body trembled.

"Are you okay?" Ein called out.

"I'm fine!" Teddy slowly got up and extended one hand toward him while gripping the handrail with the other. "Come on—if my old ass can make it, then I know you can!"

Ein took a couple of paces back and then made a running leap, but he fell short. Clutching Teddy's extended arm with a white-knuckled grip, his legs dangled perilously close to the tracks. He screamed, but the train's piercing horn drowned him out. Teddy grunted and stumbled forward, nearly pulled down with him. Throwing his whole body back, Teddy yanked as hard as he could and fell onto his rear. Ein shot up onto the catwalk and scuttled against the wall, as far from the edge as possible.

Teddy groaned and sat back up, rubbing the small of his aching back. "Jesus, kid. Are you okay?"

"Yeah," Ein said despite the rapid rise and fall of his chest. "I can't say the same about my underwear, though."

Teddy laughed and carefully stood back up. He placed one hand on the handrail and extended the other to Ein. "At least now you'll have an excuse for smelling like shit."

Ein grinned, took his hand, and got to his feet. "I guess you haven't smelled yourself lately!"

Teddy laughed. "How about we worry less about our hygiene and focus on not falling off this fucking thing?" He started edging across the catwalk and turned the corner. "Keep your back against the wall so the crosswind doesn't knock you off."

They crept along the catwalk that ran across the expanse of the locomotive and headed toward the cockpit doors. Telephone poles passed by as blurs, and bits of ice felt like steel pellets when they struck skin; Teddy figured the train had to be going at least one hundred miles per hour.

Teddy arrived at the cockpit door and turned the lever. The door flung open, and a middle-aged man wearing a FEMA officer uniform dropped the book he had been reading and bolted up from the engineer's seat, staring at Teddy in disbelief.

"What are you doing in here?"

He reached down and fumbled with a holstered pistol. Teddy snatched the man's shirt, pulled him out of the cockpit, and pushed him over the catwalk's handrail. The engineer tumbled off the locomotive and then disappeared as the train sped on. Teddy and Ein climbed into the cockpit and slammed the door shut.

"Do you know how to drive this thing?" Ein asked as he stared at the control panel.

Teddy plopped down in the engineer's seat and leaned his head back against the battered headrest. "Nah, kid, they didn't teach me that back in Texas. My train experience pretty much starts and stops at all things involving stock carriages."

Ein sat cross-legged on the floor next to him. "Then what's the plan?"

"There isn't much driving to do. We seem to be going a steady speed, and the plow in the front is taking care of the snow on the tracks." Teddy looked out the window and thought for a moment. "As long as we don't come across any camps, we can ride this thing until we see an interstate or something."

"Then what?"

"Then I hit this," Teddy said as he pointed at a large, red button labeled EMERGENCY STOP. "It seems pretty self-explanatory."

"No, I meant…afterward."

Teddy scratched his chin. "To be honest, I haven't given it much thought. I guess we can figure that out when we get to that point."

Ein looked down with a frown. "Do you think we'll go live in a city?"

"As long as there's no FEMA, sure." Teddy closed his eyes and placed his hands on his stomach. "I reckon there are plenty of free cities outside the government's control."

"What about…?" Ein's voice trailed off.

"What about what?" Teddy asked.

"Me," Ein said. "Do you think the doctor was right? Do you think I'll kill everyone I mingle with?"

Teddy opened his eyes and swiveled the chair around, staring at him with a cold, stern expression. "Kid, that doctor was full of shit—you're not sick."

"What if—?"

"You're not," Teddy interrupted. "Look, if the virus was mutating inside of you, don't you think I'd be sick from whatever new bug you could give me?"

Ein thought about it before finally nodding. "I guess you have a point."

"Then I'll hear no more of that bullshit," Teddy said firmly. "I already lost Jane and Danny. I'm not about to lose someone else."

"Who are they?" Ein asked.

"Just some people I knew." Teddy swiveled his chair back around toward the tracks ahead. "Get some sleep. We'll have a lot of walking to do when we stop."

"Sure," Ein said. "What about you?"

"I'll be fine." Teddy's stare grew vacant as he peered out into the darkness. "I don't do much sleeping these days."

They sat in silence for several minutes; Teddy thought the kid had fallen asleep until he cleared his throat.

"Teddy," Ein said.

"Yeah?"

"Thank you for everything. You didn't owe me, some stranger, anything…you didn't have to do this."

"No, kid, you don't understand. I had to do it."

"Why?" Ein asked, perplexed.

"Because I promised you." Teddy smiled faintly. "I couldn't keep my promise to them—Jane and Danny—but at least with you, I…" His voice trailed off, and he wiped an errant tear from his cheek. "Get some sleep, kid. We'll talk tomorrow."

"Okay." Suddenly, Ein looked up at him and grinned. "You'd better tell me that long story you kept referring to."

Teddy laughed. "Yeah, I will. We have nothing but time on our hands."

22

DECEMBER 21st, 1:27 P.M.

The train sat motionless some hundred miles north of Jackson, Tennessee. It blocked off a desolate county road, where a small Phillips gas station stood surrounded by frosty fields. The only other vehicle around for miles was a stalled Ford sedan that was parked on the shoulder and occupied by two frozen corpses, a couple of suitcases, and wads of crusty tissues. There was no snow on the ground, but winter's chill hung thick in the air, and the noon sun only provided a limited amount of warmth.

In the train's cockpit, a bloodstained pocketknife was on the console next to a first aid kit that had been rummaged through, its contents spread across the cabin. On the floor, amongst tattered gauze and used antiseptic wipes, were two trackers the size of two grains of rice. Small crimson droplets trailed out of the train and disappeared on the asphalt.

Further down the road, hazy in the sun's quicksilver reflection, two figures walked side by side as they headed east toward I-24.

A sound echoed across the frozen land that hadn't been heard for a very long time in those forgotten parts—the sound of laughter.

www.ingramcontent.com/pod-product-compliance
Lightning Source LLC
Chambersburg PA
CBHW040826010826
48978CB00012BB/626